THE ALIEN'S BLADE

CRAVING THE HEVEIANS
BOOK 3

ELLA BLAKE

TABLE ROCK PUBLISHING, LLC

THE ALIEN'S BLADE: CRAVING THE HEVEIANS SERIES, BOOK 3

Copyright © 2023 Ella Blake

First book edition: June 2023

Stock Art: Depositphotos

Cover Design: Ella Blake

What's worse than waking up from a hibernation cell fifty-two years after being abducted?

Nothing. No, wait—a wise-cracking alien hunk with a killer smile who doesn't let me out of his sight, that's what.

Wulfrex knows every inch of his massive space cruiser and makes it impossible for me to steal it. When I try to "borrow" one of his shuttles to get home to Earth, I find myself outsmarted by him *again* and accidentally pulled into a mission with far-reaching implications I could never have foreseen.

The beautiful human female makes my fangs and, eh, other things, ache. I know more about power converters and fusion drives than females, and Dani doesn't want to be anyone's mate—especially mine. Worse, she's an assassin, determined to get off our ship *no matter what*. Even if it means stealing aboard my shuttle as I embark on a dangerous rescue mission. She's capable with a blaster and hoards her secrets, but I *will* claim her heart.

This is book 3 in the Craving the Heveians series. I write what I love to read, so there is always consent and a HEA. Enjoy!

CHAPTER 1

Dani

I thought I knew what it felt like to wake up. I had done it many times, and not always from sleep. I'd woken up from concussions, comas, from being drugged, and once, memorably, from being held upside down for too long. Waking up from those things feels distinctly different, like flavors of ice cream, but whatever I was waking up from now, was new for me.

I lay on something soft, in an inky-black place as enveloping as a fathomless sea. I couldn't move, not even to open my eyes. Everything was heavy and warm. Reality was far, far away, except for the nagging sense that I wasn't sinking in that sea, but floating towards the surface. Part of me was afraid of that surface. Like I said, this awakening was nothing I'd felt before. The more consciousness that returned, the more afraid I became. *What happened to me?* What fresh hell would I wake up to?

There was light on the other side of my eyelids. I was beginning to see colors and shapes streak through the gray of my closed eyes, rather than black. I still couldn't open my eyes or move.

I tried to stitch together the last thing I remembered, but my memories were as fragmented and incomplete as my consciousness. I remembered how I felt though, and it wasn't good. The sour taste of regret, and feeling wrong about something I had done, made me want to retreat from that surface that was now not far above me. Soon, I would wake up from this strange sleep. I would face what was on the surface of this water, just as I'd faced every other horror in my life. And there were plenty.

This was the life of an assassin. I had been trained to expect nothing less.

Male voices drifted in, ending the silence. They moved around me and spoke a language I didn't even recognize. Feeling started to return in my hands and toes in the form of tingling. I could feel my face. The surface below me was warm, but the air above was a little cooler. I flexed my fingers and felt a soft sheet over me.

Devices hummed in the background. My mind raced for an explanation. I was in a hospital or a lab facility. There were no other reasonable explanations.

One of the males came closer. His voice was slightly gravelly and deep. The language he spoke didn't remind me of *any* Earth languages. Suddenly, a strange feeling of vertigo flowed through me, along with a sharp pain in the back of my head. I heard air hiss through my teeth, even though I still did not have full control over my body.

And then, miraculously, I could understand him.

"Is it on yet?" asked the male closest to me, to another one, farther away.

"Yes," replied the other male. "Her consciousness is returning. It's safe now to turn it on."

"If you'd done it sooner, we might have been able to talk her out of this."

"It's not safe to activate a newly installed translation device on an unconscious and cryogenically frozen patient, Wulfrex. I told you this."

The male closest to me—who had to be Wulfrex?—grunted. "If you can hear me, move something."

I assumed he was talking to me. I couldn't play dead forever, but I didn't know who these people were, or if they were dangerous or not. They knew I was awake. I gathered my courage and opened my eyes. And immediately wished I hadn't.

The individual gazing down at me was like nothing I'd ever seen before. I thought I had to still be drugged. I managed to shake my head a little. This couldn't be real. The person was male, yes, and had the general physical shape of a human, but he was *not* human. His skin was a smooth, slate gray with the slightest sheen to it. Long, wavy hair hung past his shoulders in a dark shade of blue. His eyes were a sharp contrast with his hair. They were light blue and had the slitted pupils of a cat. He was taller than most human males, at well over six feet tall, and massively muscled.

"How are you feeling?" the enormous gray alien man asked.

I opened my mouth to reply something—I had no idea what—but all that came out was a rusty croak.

The male—Wulfrex—surprised me with a broad smile. An even line of white teeth flashed, along with a pair of long and sharp canines, vampire style. "You'll be all right," he said lightly. "Just have to wait for the rest of the cryogenic chemicals to leave your body."

Cryogenics? That was why I felt so strange when returning to consciousness. I had never been cryogenically frozen before, but if what he was saying was true, something horrible had happened to me. Panic sent a rush of adrenaline and strength through my tingling body, and I surged up from the bed. Or at least I tried to.

The surface I lay on was extremely soft and warm, and my efforts to sit upright were awkward and flailing as the squishy gel foam drew me back down into its warmth. I managed to lever myself to seated, and tried to get up, only to be wrapped in a set of massive arms that held me firmly in place. Muscles on top of muscles flexed against my upper body, and a gruff voice said in my ear, "Calm down, now. Nothing is going to hurt you here."

I couldn't fight him. His bulk engulfed the top of my

body. I felt thick calluses on my skin above the sheet. It was rare that I felt this small compared to another.

"W-who are you?" I croaked.

He eased back, allowing me to sit on my own. "I am Wulfrex, and over there is Jorok, your doctor."

Doctor? Panic still rang cold and electric through my veins. But I stared calmly up at Wulfrex and schooled my reactions. No training had ever prepared me for this. "Why am I here?" My voice sounded thick, like my tongue was three sizes too big.

Wulfrex scratched the back of his head and looked down at me with a shrug. "We found you in your hibernation pod in a freighter's storage unit and brought you here. Not the easiest waking you up. How you got there…" He grinned again. "That's a mystery. What's your name, little female?"

"Dani. Dani Ling," I replied before thinking. It was my real name, or at least the only true one I knew. I blamed my befuddled state for not giving him an alias.

"And do you have any idea who put you in a cryogenically frozen state?"

I frowned up at him. "No. Last thing I remember, I was…" I cut myself off with a shake of my head. *No. Stop, stop.* I would not speak another word about it. "I don't remember much at all."

"So you don't know who she is?"

He nodded to something on my left. I turned my head to see another bed like mine, narrow and white, with a woman lying in it. She was also covered up to her shoulders in a sheet. At first, she looked dead, but horribly, I *did* recognize her. I stared in shock at the woman's face.

She lived. Of course, she lived. But only because I had spared her life, unlike that of her partner.

And now she was here with me, wherever here was. I blinked and turned away, using all of my willpower to school my features into a neutral expression as I shook my head and shrugged one shoulder. "I don't know her."

Wulfrex's eyes flickered. "A pity," he said. "We're having a difficult time waking her up."

I swallowed thickly. "Oh? That's a shame." That was a goddamn blessing if I ever heard one. As soon as that woman woke up, I was done for. On my wrist, I found a solid silver bracelet, snug enough to hug my skin, but loose enough for it to not be uncomfortable. "What's this?" I asked. "A tracking device?"

Wulfrex looked amused. "It's a *vitals* tracker." He nodded toward the dark-haired male who sat at his console about ten feet away. "So Jorok can monitor your bodily functions."

I stared at him. "So it *is* a tracker."

"Of your internal organs, yes." He was maddeningly calm, and the humor twinkling in his blue eyes was irritating. "But if you're thinking of running, you won't get far. Not that your legs are up for it, anyway."

My panic bumped up a notch. "Where am I?" On Earth, hopefully. As soon as I could get out of here, I could get to one of my safe houses and slip into a new identity.

"You are on a Heveian space cruiser in the Inrex quadrant of the galaxy." He had the grace to look a little bit apologetic. "I'm sorry to say, we're *very* far away from Earth. The only way out is through the air lock and that route, I would not advise."

I ignored most of his ramble. "The *what* quadrant?"

"Inrex. It doesn't surprise me that you haven't heard of it. There's nothing really here."

"Then why are *you* here?" I asked.

"Because we are on a mission to rescue one of our own from a location here. Also, the freighter you were found on was destined for this location."

"And what *are* you, exactly?"

"We are from the planet Heveia."

I winced. "So...you're aliens?"

"A little harsh, don't you think?" He quirked one blue eyebrow. "Don't tell me you've never seen an alien before?"

I shook my head. "Not in person. It's only been twelve years since the rift opened and visitors from other planets began arriving."

"Twelve years, eh?" His eyes sharpened. "What year is it, Dani?"

I furrowed my brow in concentration. I knew I might get this wrong, because the standard galactic timeframe was still new and not fully adopted. "I believe it's 2–28C."

Wulfrex's brows rose. "Oh, my poor little human," he said softly. "You have been in that pod for fifty-two years."

CHAPTER 2

Wulfrex

She stared up at me with her mouth agape. Dark brown eyes didn't blink as they held mine in stunned silence. "No," she rasped.

"Yes, I'm afraid."

"No." Her eyes flickered around the room. "M-maybe I got the date wrong. Maybe I—"

"Dani, it makes sense. Jorok, over here, says that the type of hibernation you were put into was meant for long-term storage. You're lucky centuries haven't passed."

I watched as denial, panic, and sheer horror over-whelmed her. She looked frantically to the door, to the woman in the other bed, and back to the door. Then she looked at me, as if sizing up the situation and gauging how to run. But the cool calculation didn't last. Her fear overrode it all, and she lunged from the bed with a strangled cry.

Her feet hit the floor and her legs crumpled. Little thing wasn't strong enough to go anywhere, yet. I gathered her into my arms before she could spill on the floor. "Easy, now," I said as she weakly fought against my hold. There was no strength in her, but her hits landed on places where, if there were strength behind them, they would hurt—neck, nose, and groin, that last one she missed because I saw it coming and shifted out of the way.

"Put her back in the bed," Jorok said. He was suddenly beside me. "She's going to hurt herself."

"Don't you dare put me back there." Frustration brimmed in Dani's eyes as she glared at me. If she had a blaster in her hand, Jorok and I would be dead. "You're the one who is going to be hurt," she snarled.

Jorok shook his head, ignoring her fury. "I need to run more tests."

"I'm thinking she won't be amenable to that," I murmured, holding down the furious, squirming female.

"Just hold her still," he said.

I pulled her closer, feeling the frantic, uneven beat of her newly awakened heart. Her breaths came ragged and shallow as her lungs worked hard for the first time in decades. My arms tightened around Dani, locking her arms and legs and preventing her from further thrashing. "I am sorry about this," I said in her ear. "But you must calm down."

"I can't stay here," she whispered urgently. "You don't understand. I—"

"There we go." Jorok placed a silver disc on the side of Dani's neck and she instantly went slack and unconscious in my arms.

"Ah, Jorok," I said. "She just woke up. Did you have to put her back to sleep again?"

"Yes," he replied, removing the metal disc and adjusting the vitals tracker on her wrist. "Her blood pressure was dangerously high. She's still very fragile, Wulfrex. Her internal organs aren't fully working yet. She could have a heart attack or a stroke in this state."

I gently placed her in the bed and arranged her limbs. Her sheet had stayed mostly intact over her, but I did catch a glimpse of sweet golden skin and a luscious hip. I gently moved a thick lock of straight black hair off her face. "She's pretty," I commented.

Jorok raised one eyebrow as he set about adjusting her intravenous tubes. "If you're looking for a mate, maybe choose one not quite as dangerous."

I grinned at him. "You caught that too? This one knows how to fight," I said, pleased. "Went right for my throat and balls."

"I saw." Jorok's jaw tightened. "Be careful. I have a feeling this one has more going on than she seems."

"What do you think she is?"

He carefully peeled back the sheet, keeping her breasts and sex covered. Humans were much more sensitive to revealing their bodies than Heveians. Even now, with the female unconscious, Jorok respected the human preferences. "Look." He pointed to several puckered scars on her abdomen. Then, he covered them back up and uncovered her left leg, on which there was a jagged scar and more of those small puckers. "This is evidence of bullet wounds."

"Bullet wounds?" My translator knew the word *bullet*, but there wasn't a Heveian equivalent.

"Projectiles that humans shoot from weapons called 'guns.' Different from blasters or plasma flares. They're quite primitive now, but they were a commonly used type of weapon on Earth before blasters and plasma flares were introduced from other species. She's from the past, Wulfrex." Jorok looked at me as if I should understand what he was saying.

But I didn't. I shook my head. "So? She got into a scrape and someone shot her. Happens all the time."

"To *us*, yes. Not to humans who live safe and stable lives on their home planet. Plus, these wounds are from different times," he said. "I have gauged her age to be twenty-nine or thirty and for that age, her bones have sustained many breaks and countless microfractures, resulting in incredible strength. On her scans, I saw multiple procedures to repair tissue internally, and also to alter her appearance. Additionally—and this is the key—I removed a chip embedded in her breastbone that would have tracked her movements." He crossed his arms. "This female did *not* live the life of an ordinary human female. That's what I'm trying to tell you."

"Could she have been military?"

He shrugged as he gazed at her in bemusement.

"Don't know. Harp was in the Earth military and lacks both the injuries and the tracking device. Dani could have been part of elite ops or some other highly dangerous role. I suppose she'll tell us when she's better."

"Hmm." I held back from sharing my observations of Dani's reaction when she'd looked at the still semi-frozen female. There was no question in my mind that she knew this woman—knew her and was afraid of her. I glanced at the other female. She was smaller in stature and more delicately built than Dani, with light brown hair and freckles over her cheeks and forehead. What about that small human had put such fear in Dani's face?

I shook my head and departed Jorok's medical lab. He had called me in to be present when Dani awoke, for the one reason he had feared—that she might awake badly. And she had. But the moment I saw the flash of fire and steel in her eyes as they locked on mine, I was intrigued. She was a puzzle to unravel, and there was nothing I found more exciting than a project that *might* result in an explosion.

CHAPTER 3

Dani

When I woke up again, I was more prepared for what to expect. The feelings were the same—rising to the surface of a warm, dark sea. But this time, I knew what was happening and what I would wake up to. Knowing brought with it fresh numbness creeping up my limbs and twisting my stomach in a roiled knot.

Fifty-two years? I squeezed my eyes shut. The people who'd hired me were probably dead. They'd been old to begin with. My handlers, the agency I worked for, had long since written me off. I thought about the woman Jorok hadn't been able to wake up, yet—Claire. She'd seen what I'd done. She knew what I was. If it weren't for her, I could deny my entire past and start over.

With reluctance, I opened my eyes a second time.

Although I was only looking at the ceiling, I knew I was in a new room. This one was warmer. The light was soft on a warm gray ceiling and the air reminded me of tea and honey.

I drew in a deep breath and pushed myself up to sitting, closing my eyes again as my muscles ached and my joints popped and cracked. I opened my eyes again. "Gah!"

I wasn't alone. Three women sat on my bed, arranged as if they had been there waiting for a while.

"Hi," said one, a short, friendly-looking woman with tan skin and red tips to her black hair. She had a warm smile on her face. "Welcome back."

"Um. Hello," I said, trying to size up these women as quickly and efficiently as possible.

The black- and red-haired woman placed her hand on her chest. "I'm Kora. This, here, is Harp, and this is Arria."

The one named Harp was a very beautiful brown-skinned woman with curly hair and a twinkle to her dark eyes. "Hey there," she said. "Your name is Dani, right?"

"That's right." They were all dressed comfortably. They looked happy, which was strange in itself. Unless… "Am I still on the spaceship?"

"You are," replied the third woman, the one named Arria. She was a petite woman with long, light hair and was paler than the other two. There was a sharp intelligence to her eyes. "How are you feeling?"

That was a loaded question if I ever heard one. How was I feeling? "A little of everything, I think."

She nodded sagely. "We know the feeling."

Did they? I doubted any of these three women had any idea how I felt. None of them looked like they had a job that sometimes involved killing people. I smiled politely. "Were you three frozen, too?"

"No, we were abducted and thrown in an alien prison," Harp replied. "On a different alien ship. These guys—the Heveians—rescued us."

"Did they?" Rescued them, my foot. More like imprisoned them and made them think they were rescued and should be so grateful for—

"They tell us you were frozen for fifty-two years," said Kora. "A lot has changed since then. On Earth, that is."

I had no doubt about that. "The convergence, the rift, and all that, was still pretty new last I remember. Now, I guess, being abducted by aliens is commonplace."

Harp laughed. "It's *not* commonplace, but it happened to all of us in this room." She cocked her head. "What's your story?"

"Story?"

"Yeah," said Harp. "Do you remember being taken? What was your life like before they abducted you and put you in that cryogenic pod?"

Those were questions I would not answer. Not honestly, anyway. "My life was a lot more boring than this," I said lightly, with a breezy wave of my hand, as if

brushing off the dullness of my past. "I was a consultant. Not that any of it matters now." The ironic truth
was it *didn't* matter now. I was here, and here was
where I needed to start figuring a path forward.

I looked down to see myself dressed in a comfortable, loose-fitting tunic. Under the sheet, I was wearing
leggings. Both garments were made of a soft, buttery
material. "How did I get these?"

Kora pointed at my shirt. "We made you some
clothes. Well, we didn't actually *make* them, but there's a
machine here that can produce just about anything you
want, so we made you a few outfits that should be
comfortable as you recover."

"That's thoughtful of you," I said. "Thank you." The
outfit was comfortable and easy to move in. I stretched
and found the metal bracelet still on my wrist. I tried to
pull it off but couldn't even find a seam to pry my
fingernail into. "Why do I still have to wear this?" I
asked sharply.

"Jorok said he wanted you to wear that a little
longer, just to make sure that your vital signs stay
stable," said Arria. "Sometimes, there can be latent
trauma to the body following cryogenic freezing."

"I see. I feel fine, though. Almost normal." I would
get the tracking bracelet off one way or another, and I
was going to have to deal with these women. They were
nice. Perhaps I could find out more about the males
running the ship, and more importantly, how to get off
it and back to Earth. "So what are these aliens like?" I
asked. "Do you trust them?"

Harp and Kora exchanged a look and started laughing.

"Oh, we trust them," said Harp. "Kora and I are with two of them."

"What do you mean, 'with'?"

"As in, they're our partners. It sounds a little strange, doesn't it?" Kora winced. "We've been here a while. Gone through a lot. Some romance bloomed." She smiled. "Don't worry. They don't force themselves on us. The Heveians are just sexy as hell."

"True," said Harp. "In fact, my guy, Drave, took some convincing. Now, he's all mine." She crossed her arms and leaned back with a satisfied look.

I looked at Arria. "Do you have an alien boyfriend, too?" I asked. It came out sounding a little tart, despite trying to hide my horror at this "romance" revelation.

Arria shook her head. "I prefer to be on my own."

At last, some sensible talk.

Harp rolled her eyes and shook her head. "The captain has it bad for our sweet little genius, here."

Arria shook her head. "Nonsense."

Harp shrugged, but looked smug. "Hardly matters either way, if you're not interested."

Arria lifted one narrow shoulder. "I didn't say I wasn't interested, just that I prefer to be on my own."

Harp winked at Arria. "I don't know how you can resist that big, hot—"

"Anyway," Kora cut in with an amused look at Harp. "We didn't come here to brag about our sex lives. We came to welcome you, and see what we could do to make you comfortable. Is there anything you need? I'm sure you have a lot of questions."

I did. So many that I couldn't pick one to start with. "So, you all just...fell in love with these guys? After they abducted you?"

"No, no. They didn't abduct us," Kora said. "They rescued us from an alien prison, which was really horrible, I might add. We almost died there."

"And you aren't worried that maybe...you were manipulated a little bit?" I swallowed, well aware that I was wading into dangerous territory. Manipulated people never easily admitted that they were being manipulated.

"Do we seem manipulated to you?" Harp asked with one raised brow.

"No, you don't *seem* it," I replied carefully. "But this whole situation just seems a little like brainwashing, don't you think? Big, handsome alien guys whisk you off your feet and, boom, you're in love." I looked around at the three of them, knowing it was probably a mistake to say these things, but it looked like these alien males had some sort of mind-control skills, or perhaps devices that caused women to *think* they'd fallen in love with them. I couldn't come up with a different likelihood. Who just fell in love like that, unless they were being manipulated?

"Trust me, none of us are brainwashed." Kora reached out and patted my knee. "We are very much in control of our own minds. But I get why you'd wonder about that."

I looked at Arria, the only one who seemed to have not succumbed to the brainwashing. "It seems like Stockholm syndrome to me."

Arria nodded, looking sympathetic. "Honestly, I would probably have the same thoughts if I were you, walking into this and meeting us for the first time. But I can tell you with certainty that no one here has Stockholm syndrome. No one is falling in love with their abusers because there's no abuse going on."

I nodded and awkwardly moved the conversation away from their love lives to more mundane matters. I asked about food and the bathroom. Apparently, they had full access to the ship, to go anywhere they wanted. I learned that Kora had been a teacher before she'd been abducted, Harp had been in the military, and Arria, well, she seemed reluctant to talk about her past, but indicated that her family had been in a cult of some sort. That put her not in a different situation than she'd been in before, but I refrained from saying that.

The women seemed happy, friendly, and overall very pleasant. Altogether, those things made me mistrustful of them. I promised myself not to say anything to them of note. There would be no confiding in these women. They would just inform their alien masters.

Just as Arria was finishing telling me about the joys of the swimming pool on the ship, the door slid open and a robot walked inside.

A real robot—not the staggering, awkward things in experimental labs that couldn't hold a cup of water in their clawed grips. I stared at the thing. The robot walked forward almost elegantly, with a natural, smooth gait that was utterly unnerving. It walked on slender legs, like a human, had a torso and two narrow arms. It was made of some sort of brass-like metal that shined and gleamed as if it were polished daily. Its head was a smooth egg shape with a single black circle in the center like an eye. I scrambled back, pressing myself against the headboard.

"Don't be afraid," said Arria in her gentle, soft voice. "That's just Hoc. Have you come to meet Dani, Hoc?"

"Why, yes, I have. Greetings, Dani Ling," said the robot in a male-sounding digital voice. "Welcome to the Heveian space cruiser. I am Hoc, cybot assistant. If you need anything, do not hesitate to summon me."

I stared at it, my eyes frozen wide open in fear.

"Oh, that's right," said Harp. "Cybots were after your time. You've never seen one of these before."

I shook my head, unable to tear my gaze away from the very sentient and very dangerous robot. "No. Never have."

"Cybots are very common, now," Harp explained. "On Earth, they help with lots of things. Hoc, here, was a bartender bot on a space outpost before he got a new body and joined this crew."

I did not care about this creature's body or what his function was now or in the past. The fact that they had professions was mind-blowing in itself. I just wanted it away from me. "Okay," I said shakily. "You know

THE ALIEN'S BLADE   23

what? I think all this has worn me out. Would you all mind if I took a nap?"

"Of course not," said Kora, rising to her feet. "How silly of us. We should've realized you'd still be tired."

The women got up and left with goodbyes. Kora gave me a hug, which I did not want, but I returned it anyway. I didn't trust them, but I also didn't want to alienate them.

When the room was empty, I got out of bed, testing the strength in my legs. I was still slightly rubbery in the knees, but I could walk. The first thing I did was search every corner of the room. Every compartment, shelf, and drawer. If it could hold a weapon or a listening device, I searched it. I found no obvious listening devices, but who knew what new technology these aliens possessed? I located some metal eating utensils that could be used as weapons, if I needed them.

Who was I kidding? I would need them.

On the wall was a large screen that was black, but when I approached it, it woke up and revealed itself as an interface—a vast array of symbols and alien letters that looked like something out of a science-fictional movie. I was still trying to figure out how to navigate it when a prompt suddenly popped up on the screen.

A smooth, female voice spoke from the screen. For a second, I didn't understand it, but then there was a gentle ache in the back of my head, and the device they'd implanted there kicked in. A translation device, put inside my brain without my permission. If there was ever any reason to worry, *there* was one.

"What would you like to see?"

I hesitated for a moment, unsure of what to do. Then I took a deep breath and asked, "Can I see a plan of the ship?"

To my shock, schematics of the space cruiser appeared on the screen in more detail than I could have imagined. I leaned forward and began to study what I saw. If I was going to find a way off the ship, I needed to know every corner of it. Top to bottom. I studied the plan, looking for any weaknesses or openings I could exploit. After a few moments, I had a good sense of the layout and I began to formulate a plan.

I had been studying the plans for hours and my stomach was starting to remind me that I hadn't eaten in, well, years, which was strange. I couldn't remember the last time I had felt so hungry.

Kora had explained to me that the ship had a machine built into the wall, programmed to dispense food items. Nervously, I made my way to it and found the machine in question. It was simple to operate, though the menu was lacking in variety. It dispensed some bland-tasting bars. They were the only things it was programmed to make for me right now. Apparently, my stomach could handle only simple foods for a while. I was just relieved I had something to eat without having to ask for help.

As I ate the bars, I wondered what other surprises the ship held in store for me. I didn't plan to be here long enough to get used to this strange new environment, but I still had much to explore and learn if I was going to get home. I took a few more bites of the bars, feeling my stomach slowly fill with sustenance.

After eating them, and having a drink of water, I tucked the fork and knife I'd found in my pockets and went to the door. I half expected it to be locked. I was surprised to see it slide open at my touch.

With the schematic of the ship still fresh on my mind, I stepped swiftly out of my room to begin my search of the ship, and the ultimate goal—getting off of it—and slammed straight into a broad chest. I looked up to see Wulfrex grinning down at me. "Going somewhere, little female?"

CHAPTER 4

Wulfrex

My arms automatically closed around her. I breathed in deeply, filling my senses with her scent. She had the smell of freshly made clothes from the fabricator. Gathering her close felt as natural as breathing. I should have worried about that, since her muscles immediately stiffened and her eyes flashed up at me with a distinctly unwelcome gleam.

"I'm five foot ten," she said crisply. "I'm hardly little."

"You're little to me," I said. "And you're most definitely female." I was becoming more and more aware of that, now that she was well.

She was taller than the other women here. Her bones were strong, as were her muscles. Still, she had a lovely curvy shape to her that made my cock tighten and my fangs ache. I was attracted to this female. She was beautiful, but so were the other women. Something about Dani drew me in, in a way no other female ever had.

"You can let me go now," she said.

I grinned down at her, taking in the shape of her features. The annoyed arch of her brow, her sexy, heavy-lidded eyes, delicate nose, and pert, pouty mouth. All of it was set in a heart-shaped face.

I thought about the wounds her medical scans had revealed. All of those injuries. What did they mean? "Are you sure you want me to? You fit quite nicely here, I think."

I was about to let her go, but before I could comply, she shifted a leg and hooked it behind my knee. She yanked with her leg and I had to lift my foot. I didn't fall on the floor. My own bulk and natural balance had saved me from that humiliation, but I released her in the process.

She crossed her arms and raised one brow. "You're the first one I've done that to who hasn't found himself flat on his back," she said. "Congratulations."

I spread my arms in a dramatic fashion and bowed. "It's an honor to be your first," I said. "Is that a human courtship move, or were you just happy to see me?"

Her eyes narrowed. Her lips thinned. "It's standard self-defense. You're just so bulky, my leg couldn't reach around and take out both of your knees."

"Nevermind," I said with the shake of my head.

"Harp told me a version of that joke. I still don't quite get it."

"I don't get it either." She touched the back of her head. "Maybe this thing you people put inside my brain without asking me is malfunctioning."

"Oh." So she was displeased about that. "We couldn't ask you because you wouldn't have understood anything we said."

"Don't you have three humans at your command?"

I made a confused face at that as I tried to understand what she meant. "At our command? If you're referring to Harp, Kora and Arria, they are at no one's command. They would've helped out, though, if they could." I tapped a finger on her forehead, which she batted away. "But if you remember, which you obviously don't, you were unconscious. Jorok had to make an executive decision. We needed to be able to communicate with you. If it helps, everyone on Earth has these now."

She bunched up her shoulders, but nodded. "I don't like being tracked."

I sighed. Dani was angry. Angry at something I probably couldn't fix. "On behalf of the crew of this ship, I apologize for implanting a translator device in your brain without your permission. There. Is that better?"

"Yes, actually."

"Good." I swept my arm out towards the hall, which curved out in front of us. There were a few doors, and some that were only indentions where a door would be.

There were no windows, only glass panels that glowed with a soft light. "Would you like me to show you around the ship?"

"Do you mean a tour?" She looked suspicious.

"Yes. You should know your way around since you're going to be here for a while."

She nodded curtly. "Yes, please. I would like to learn everything about this ship."

I held out my arm, elbow out, the way I had seen Ryland and Drave do for their human mates. Apparently, Hoc had coached them a little on human interactions. This was something human men did when escorting a woman somewhere.

Dani looked at my elbow for a moment. I thought for sure she would refuse my offer, but then her gaze flickered up to mine, and that cold mask cracked just a little. I saw uncertainty and a slice of vulnerability there that made my interest in her flare.

She reached out, with adorable hesitation, then her fingers curled around the crook of my arm. "Okay," she said. "But I just want you to know something right now."

"What's that?" I asked, enjoying the zing of sensation that shot out over my skin from the point where she touched me.

"It's not going to work on me."

"What's not going to work on you?"

She shook her head vehemently. "You may be funny and very impressive to look at, but I will not be falling in love with you under any circumstances."

I blinked down at her. "You think I'm funny?"

"That's what you're taking away from my statement?"

"Well, I know I'm impressive," I said. "But I'm pleased to know you admire my sense of humor."

"I don't—" She cut off with a deep breath, then waved a finger in the air. "Look. Whatever tricks, magic, or mind games you Heveians played on Kora and Harp to enthrall them, it won't work on me. I've been trained to see through all of that."

I stared at her for a moment before bursting out laughing. "You think Ryland and Drave did something to make their mates fall for them?" I could not stop laughing. I dislodged her hand from my elbow as I bent over.

"Why are you laughing?" She sounded exasperated.

"Wait until you meet Drave, then repeat that state-ment with a straight face. He's about as warm and fuzzy as a block of ice. And Ryland has about as much natural charisma as an air lock." I gathered myself and wiped away a tear. "The idea of either of them working some sort of magic to make Harp and Kora fall in love with them is just too funny. Your sense of humor is nothing to sniff at."

"I wasn't trying to be funny."

If I didn't cut it out, I'd get a foot to the back of my knee again, and this time, she'd likely land the move better and I would be down on my arse. I faced her, pressed my palms together and schooled my features to something appropriately serious. "Okay, Dani. I promise you, nobody is doing tricks or magic on anyone on this ship. And I have no plans to manipulate you in any way. We are not your enemy."

She looked up at me with uncertainty. "Sometimes, it's hard to know who our enemies are."

I lifted her hands, which had fallen slack at her side, and kissed her knuckles. She didn't pull away and I took that as a win. I stepped to her side and tucked her hand back into the crook of my arm. "With me, what you see is what you get."

"I would like to believe that." Her voice was a harsh whisper and I wondered if all those scars on her body had matching ones in her mind.

"Let me show you our ship," I said. "I personally work on it every day."

"You do?"

"Yes." I nodded proudly. "I'm the chief engineer. Anything goes wrong, I'm on it. I know every bit of this ship, how it works, how to fix it, and how to make it run better. I've always been a bit of a nerd like that." I grinned down at her. "Did I use that word right?"

"What? Nerd?" One corner of her mouth reluctantly tipped upwards. "Yes. You did." Her gaze ran up and down me, frankly assessing. "I will admit, that surprises me."

"That I'm a nerd?"

She actually let out a chuckle. "That you're the chief engineer. Frankly, you look like you spend all your time in the gym."

"Oh, this magnificence?" I gestured to my body,

which was generously layered with muscles. "The finest Heveian genetics, as my father would tell you. And I do enjoy sparring in the training room with Ryland."

"And so humble," she murmured with that slight smile still in place.

I would win this female over. "Now, shall we?" I nodded forward. "Care to see where you'll be living for a while?"

She flourished a hand. "Lead on, nerd."

CHAPTER 5

Dani

Wulfrex showed me all over the ship. He was quite proud of this place, his home. He showed off the special details like safety precautions at junction points and special lighting that corresponded to day and night cycles. We stopped at the training room, which seemed surprisingly large for being on a ship in space. A blue-haired Heveian was giving sword lessons to twelve alien beings when we arrived.

"That is Ryland," said Wulfrex. "Ryland Crex, our chief security officer."

"And who are all those other...creatures?"

Wulfrex cocked his head. "I wouldn't call them creatures. They are part of the crew and they come from all corners of the galaxy. All of them highly specialized at their jobs." He slanted me a look. "You had no idea there were so many types of beings in your galactic neighborhood, did you?"

I shook my head, staring in awe at the different-shaped life forms standing in a row facing Ryland, concentrating on their lesson. There was a being no more than a foot tall and another one twice my height. One had four legs and another had giant compound eyes like an Earth fly.

"And this isn't even the beginning. There are life forms in this galaxy that would amaze you," he said. "Some don't breathe oxygen. Some don't breathe at all. Some are gas or liquid based, and there are even some that are pure energy and can take any shape they like."

"Wow," I breathed. "How many crew members are on this ship?"

"We have fifty-seven crew members, not including the five of us Heveians and three—no, now five —humans."

"And you pay them?"

He nodded. "Galactic credits. A good fee, I'll add. We don't like a lot of turnover, for obvious reasons. And we're not exactly on all the registries, if you know what I mean."

"I don't know what you mean." We backed away from the training room and Wulfrex quietly closed the door. "Well, we did some work for hire for a while. Mostly retrieving stolen goods, disrupting the trade routes of certain entities, and ambushing freighters now and then to steal their cargo."

My eyes went wide. "Oh my god, you're pirates."

"No, we are not." He drew in a breath and paused. "Well, not anymore. Our home planet went under attack by a group called the UCP, or the United Coalition for Peace, which is a load of shit, to use your human term. They want the power crystals under the surface of our planet, Heveia. They'll do anything to get it, including letting loose a disease that would have wiped out our population, if a cure had not been found in time."

I stared, transfixed as memories pinged in my head. "You're serious? The UCP let loose a pathogen that killed your people?"

His eyes sharpened. "They did. Are you familiar with the UCP?"

I frowned. "I feel like I've heard that name. People I used to work for may have mentioned them."

The light, carefree part of him vanished and in its place was an intense male, acutely tuned in to every word I said. And I realized, belatedly, that I'd said too much.

"If you did hear about the UCP, then they were at your planet from almost the beginning, when sublight tunnels opened up in your sector. They wasted no time in scoping out your system." He shook his head. "We should've known."

"I'm not exactly sure what I heard," I said, trying to backpedal.

"Who did you work for, exactly?" he asked.

I shrugged. "Lots of different people," I replied vaguely. "I was a consultant."

"What did you consult about?"

"It doesn't matter anymore. I'm here—far, *far* from Earth, and all the people I ever worked with are dead now anyway, probably." I started to walk off, just to get out of this line of questioning. I turned back towards Wulfrex, who stood where he was, gazing at me thoughtfully. "Are we going?" I asked. "We haven't seen everything, have we?"

He opened his mouth to say something, then closed it with a quick shake of his head, clearly changing his mind about questioning me further.

Maybe he thought he could work on me later. It wouldn't happen. These people could never know what I did. As we moved on, Wulfrex was slightly less cheerful.

The main deck was a large oval. One side of the room featured a curved bank of consoles with podlike seats. There was a huge bank of monitors and computer screens lining the wall. The floor was cushioned and softly lit, with big, comfortable-looking chairs all around. Different life forms, like the ones I'd seen in the training room, were positioned at stations.

A wall of windows looking out into the dark expanse of space dominated the other wall. I could hear the ship humming, the tapping of fingers on screens, and the creak of seats as staff members shifted. The air inside was cool and clean, smelling just faintly of warm electronics.

I recognized the captain immediately. He stood in the center, leaning over a tabletop screen with his arms crossed. There was a sense of weight and responsibility to him that wasn't quite matched in anybody else. At one of the pods, which had a curved screen that went right over top of it, sat a Heveian with the lightest blue hair I'd seen and a ruggedly masculine frame. He had a headset on that covered one ear as his hands flew over the screen before him. In the next pod over sat Harp, whom I recognized immediately. She wore the same type of headset, and she turned to the male next to her and said something. He looked at her with a smirk and said something back.

I watched them banter for a moment, finding the interaction interesting. She seemed to be teasing him about something, and he was doing his best not to react, but clearly enjoying it. Finally, she leaned over from her pod and lightly whacked his arm. He leaned over at her, and I saw him mouth back something like, *get back to work, or I'll fire you,* to which she laughed out loud and they both settled back into their screens.

The captain strode over to us. He was not as tall or bulky as Wulfrex, and he appeared to be the oldest of them. His hair was a lighter blue than Wulfrex's, and his eyes lacked any twinkle of humor. "It is a pleasure to meet you, Dani. Or would you prefer Ms. Ling?"

He reached for a hand, and I gave it to him. "Dani is fine."

He bowed over it without kissing my knuckles, thank goodness, and then released it formally and politely, unlike any of Wulfrex's behavior so far. "It's a relief to see you up and about. I am Axlos, captain of the cruiser." He gestured towards the icy-haired male in the pod. "Over there is Drave, our communications officer. You have already met Harp."

Drave looked up and nodded cooly towards me. Harp waved and smiled.

"Aside from Ryland, you have made the acquaintance of all of the senior officers on the ship. I wish our introduction had not been so stressful for you. As with the other humans, no one can be prepared for an abduction."

I took in his words, weighing them and trying to gauge this male, who literally held my life in his hands. One word, and the captain had the authority to toss me out into space.

"Thank you for your hospitality," I said just as formally. "It is a relief to be up and about." My gaze shifted to a curved wall of windows. "It looks so big out there," I said. Outside that window, space stretched fathomless and black, dotted with brilliant stars.

"It's bigger than you think it is, when you've spent your whole life on a planet's surface, looking up," said Axlos. "It was a jolt for us, as well, the first time we went out on the ship."

"Stole it, you mean," said Wulfrex with a grin. "We did, you know. Nicked it right off the landing pad from the royal hangar. Got us exiled."

"Yes, it did," said Axlos. "Fortunately, the new crown prince pardoned us." He smiled apologetically. "We are *not* outlaws."

I held up my hands. "I'm not judging." Little did

they know I had more reason to worry about their judgment than they ever did about mine. "Wulfrex said that we are in this area to rescue a fellow Heveian, and that the other woman who is frozen and I were supposed to be sent here."

Axlos nodded. "Correct. We hope to retrieve one of our own and solve the mystery of what your fate would have been. We should be arriving at the mine soon, and after we're done there, we will see about a return trip to Heveia, where our crown prince has a human crown princess." Axlos smiled at me, clearly hoping this information would please me. It did not. This crown princess was just another brainwashed woman to contend with. And this one, was in a position of power.

"We will let you get back to your work," Wulfrex interjected. "I was just showing Dani around the ship." He looked at me. "And you must be getting tired. I'll bring you back to your room."

I nodded. I actually *was* getting tired. It would take a little time for my full strength and stamina to return.

Wulfrex was a bit broody on the way back. A glance up revealed a furrowed brow and a tight jaw. We reached my room, which I now remembered how to get to alone. I stopped him with a hand to his arm.

"What is it?" I asked. "If you have something to say, get it out."

"Fine." He stopped sharply and turned to me. "Who are you, really?"

I blinked up at him, feigning confusion. "I don't know what you mean."

"Where were you when you were abducted?"

"The moon," I said without hesitation. "As in, Earth's moon. We only have one."

"And what were you doing there?"

"I told you. I was a consultant. I was consulting." Wow, where was my finesse? My smooth delivery? All of it vanished when faced with this male.

"On what?" I could hear the frustration in his voice.

I reached up and patted his cheek with the goal of setting him off balance. "Absolutely nothing that would interest you," I responded. "Just business."

His eyes flickered. He leaned slightly into my touch, just enough for me to feel the high, rugged cheekbones beneath my fingers. He really was absurdly handsome. His nose was well shaped, except for a slight bend in it where he must have been on the wrong end of a fist. His eyebrows winged upwards on the edges, making him look very much the part of a pirate. He even had a scar running down the side of his forehead and bisecting one brow. His full lips were set in a natural curl, as if he found everything around him mildly amusing. And his jawline—sweet lord, Wulfrex could crack nuts on his jaw.

He was cut and sculpted like something out of a goddamn dream. It really actually made sense that these women fell in love with these males. They were over-the-top handsome and, I had to admit, terribly charming.

A huge, calloused hand covered mine. Sensations

zinged up my arm, sending warmth throughout my body.

Wulfrex blinked down at me, eyes languid and dark. "What are you keeping from me?" he asked softly.

My pulse fluttered. It felt like a bird was flapping in my ribs, trying to get out. "I'm sorry," I said. "There are some things I just can't talk about."

"Why not?"

"Because trust is something that has to be earned in my world."

"In mine, too," he said. "But bear in mind that if your secrets pose a threat to anyone on this ship, it's a problem. For you. For all of us."

"I know." I struggled not to show my nerves. If they knew that I'd been assigned to murder the partner of the woman who was currently in the medical lab still unconscious—and that I'd completed my assignment— would they lock me up? Would they let me live at all?

He leaned close. "I *will* get your secrets out of you eventually." The glint was back, mixed with the edge of arousal. That large hand covering mine closed around my fingers and lifted my hand off his cheek. He brought my palm to his lips and pressed a kiss there.

My blasted body betrayed me with an uneven gasp as his mouth seared my skin. *Christ*, these males were potent. Did they have special pheromones, or was I just as susceptible as the other women here?

I pulled my hand away with a shaky sigh. I felt marked, branded somehow. My fingers closed in a fist as my hand throbbed. "We'll see," I pushed out in a rasp.

He gave me a rakish grin, flicked his thumb over my chin, and sauntered away as if nothing had happened. As if I wasn't standing there now, dragging in ragged breaths and wondering if my heart was going to break out of my chest and go running after him.

I entered my room in a bad mood. How weak was I to allow that big alien to push my buttons like that?

"Hi," said a soft voice.

I looked up sharply to see Arria there. I *should've* seen her. I should've looked. I was also getting soft in my ability to monitor my surroundings at all times. This annoying male had me all shaken up. "Sorry. I didn't see you there." My voice sounded clipped. My words, sharp.

"It's okay," she said. "We're sharing this room now, just so you know." She was sitting on one of the stuffed chairs in the common area of the room. "I stayed somewhere else to give you a chance to rest and settle in, but Drave does not like sleeping on the couch."

"You stayed with Harp?" I asked.

She nodded. "There's limited space in the cruiser, with all the crew. Not a lot of guest spaces."

"So all three of you stayed here before they…"

"Paired off?" She nodded with a smile. "That's right. It was like a slumber party every night. Kora snores."

I snorted out a chuckle. My foul mood faded away with the easy conversation. "So tell me, Arria, how did *you* avoid falling for one of these aliens? I met Captain Axlos." I raised one brow. "He is impressive."

"He is, isn't he?" Arria had a cup of tea in her hands and she sipped it thoughtfully. "I have difficulty being comfortable around men in power," she said. "It's a result of my past and a part I haven't worked through, yet. I don't like relying on anyone and I'm still trying to figure out who I am."

"So, you like him, but his position makes you uneasy?"

"That sounds accurate. He's been very nice, and he has not in any way pushed himself on me. I probably wouldn't even know of his interest if it weren't for Kora and Harp."

This was interesting. The way she talked, it sounded as if this could be any relationship, any interaction on Earth between girlfriends. Which was something I'd never had, growing up as I did. "I wonder if you and I have more in common than we think," I mused out loud.

"You grew up in a fundamentalist cult that used torture as discipline and didn't allow women to be educated?"

"Oh." That brought me up short. "No. But I didn't grow up in a normal family, and there was plenty of discipline that wouldn't be considered legal." Punishments where I was raised were tests of endurance— staying underwater until you nearly passed out, enduring blizzards with nothing but a bathrobe, being forced to stay awake for days at a time. It was about survival, and that didn't even touch on the training to do the more gruesome tasks.

I headed to my bed, feeling tired. There was a divider up between the beds for some privacy. I sat on the edge of my bed, which went beyond comfortable, really. These beds seemed to know where your body needed support and where it needed softness and delivered it to just those spots. Just sitting on it made me sleepy. "I understand the need to rely only on yourself."

Arria nodded, studying me over the rim of her mug. "Only, on a ship like this, that's impossible. It's like a little village where everyone has unique skills. Everyone has to lean on everybody else, and trust that we will take care of each other." Her dark eyes cleared. "It's difficult, sometimes."

"It is." Just saying those two words felt like a brick being lifted off my chest. Arria wasn't an assassin. She hadn't been raised from childhood to feel guiltless when taking a life. She had not been taught a hundred ways to kill someone and a thousand ways to lie. But I sensed she knew a bit of my struggle because she shared elements of it herself.

"It'll be okay, Dani," Arria said.

"Are you really a genius, like Harp said you were?"

She shrugged a shoulder indifferently. "I learned the Heveian language in a couple of weeks, so they had me take some IQ assessment tests. They came back high." She shook her head. "It's kind of funny."

"How so?"

"I wasn't allowed to go to school on Earth, yet here I

am on a spaceship in the middle of nowhere with aliens and I'm allowed to be whoever I want to be." She shrugged again. "It's just funny that it took being abducted by aliens and almost dying in a horrible cell, to come to a place where I could be free."

As I crawled into bed and pulled the covers over me, I thought about her words.

To be free.

I'd never thought about what that meant. I hadn't even considered it as a possibility for me. And the only thing preventing me from being free was the woman still asleep in the medical lab.

I fell asleep with the hand Wulfrex kissed tucked between my breasts and my face still tingling where those thick fingers had brushed.

Who was I? Who was I without my guns and training and a mission?

I would have to find out, or the secrets of my past would swallow me whole.

CHAPTER 6

Wulfrex

"What do you think of the new female?" Drave asked the question as we sat in our lounge, just the two of us. He was contemplating a fermented beverage that smelled slightly sour to me, as we sat in thick chairs with a low, flat table between us. The lounge was small, but welcoming. We had designed the small, private lounge for the five of us Heveians to remind us of our home planet. The walls were dark brown, the lighting was warm, and the furniture was heavy and richly colored, but practical. We lived underground, for the most part, on Heveia, due to the harsh surface conditions. This place, which had previously been a storage vault, replicated the effect.

Still, his question caught me off guard. Drave had a way of behaving like he didn't care what went on around him, but in actuality, he missed nothing. Which meant he had noticed something between Dani and me. "I think she is remarkable," I answered honestly. "But also that she's hiding something."

Drave nodded. "Fair assessment. The other women suspect she's hiding something, but they haven't the faintest idea what."

"She has some fighting skills," I remarked. "And she clearly doesn't trust us."

"No, she thinks we have somehow brainwashed the other human females."

"Brainwashed?" I asked. "What does that mean?"

"As it was explained to me, it means tricking or manipulating someone into doing something they wouldn't ordinarily do, or that is against their own best interests." Drave shrugged. "That's the best I can figure out. Dani thinks we release some pheromones or have some sort of special ability to make the females fall in love with us." He snorted and shook his head. "The idea of Harp being obedient is laughable."

I couldn't imagine it either. Drave's mate was smart and opinionated, and definitely had her own mind about things. "If we give out pheromones, I'm not aware of it."

"We don't," Drave said flatly. "But for Dani to think we do, indicates to me that she doesn't give the benefit of the doubt. And doesn't trust human emotions."

I considered telling him what Dani had mentioned about how the UCP was familiar to her, but I thought better of it. Until I knew more about her, I would keep some of her secrets. And I did not want my friends to treat her with suspicion, especially knowing how frightened she probably was being here.

"Well, whatever she's hiding, it can't be that bad," said Drave, taking another sip from his cup. "She's a human who was captured some fifty-two years ago. Anything she might've done is irrelevant now."

I certainly hoped that was true. I played with my own drink, a bitter ale made in the style of the Heveian mountain dwellers. Or, at least, the closest to it the replicators could make. "She knows the other female who was in stasis with her," I said.

Drave raised one eyebrow. "You suspect this, or you *know* it?"

"Suspect," I replied. "It was the way she reacted when she saw the other female. She looked surprised and did not appear pleased to see her. In fact, she looked afraid."

"She denied knowing this female?" Drave asked.

I nodded. "And then she wouldn't look at her."

"Interesting." Drave took another sip. "But it proves nothing. You'll have to wait and see if you can get more information from her."

"I'll work on that."

Drave smirked. "I bet you will."

I raised an eyebrow at him. "What does that mean?"

"It means you are more than a little intrigued. Perhaps she is the one brainwashing you?" Drave said this with a smirk and I knew he was joking.

No one was brainwashing anyone. I was simply

attracted to Dani. I shrugged. "Brainwashed, no. Attracted, yes. And I suspect she is attracted to me, too. Or, at least, she would be, if she could work through her suspicions."

"It's possible she doesn't like you," said Drave.

"Nonsense." I shook my head and knocked back a big swallow of ale. "Everyone likes me."

Drave chuckled and shook his head. "Annoyingly enough, this is true. But there's a difference between liking you and wanting to rut with you."

I winced. "True enough."

Just then, the sensor device I wore on my ear pinged. With a grunt, I turned over my wrist and regarded the wide *plastoid* device I wore there. It contained an interface screen that was necessary since the ship's functions were my responsibility.

I read the alert with a frown. "I need to go," I said. "There's a biological entity in the passageways near thruster tubes."

"Another *cagrot* infestation?" asked Drave. "Every time we stop for supplies it seems we pick up those eggs and they hatch. I thought the irradiator was supposed to destroy them."

I watched the little dot on the map on my screen, showing me the heat signature of the biological entity that was running amok in sensitive areas of the ship. Something about its movements didn't remind me of *cagrots*. "Possibly." I rose, finishing off my drink in one swallow, then dropping the cup into the recycler. "I need to go check it out."

Drave took another contemplative sip of his drink. "You think it's her, don't you?"

"What would a human be doing, poking around in the maintenance areas of this ship?"

Drave raised his glass. "I'm sure you'll find out."

———

I moved through the cruiser, which I could navigate backwards with my eyes closed, following the signal to where the breach was.

I found an access panel carefully closed, but with the slightest of cracks—perfect for anyone trying to make a quick entrance and exit without being caught. I slipped inside. It was dark in these areas, lit by only the dimmest of lights, and it was cold. We were close to the outer panels, all that separated us from the frigid void of space. Here, the ship was a mass of tubing, power transfers, and all the other parts that went into making the space cruiser operate. It was where I spent a substantial part of my day, but other than my small crew of engineers, no one came in here. I wound my way through the tight passages and sharp angles, avoiding jutting metal and *plastoid* beams that crowded the space.

I listened hard and detected the sounds of movement ahead. Despite my size, I could move very quietly when I wanted to, and this time, I wanted to. I shifted through the passages, and then, I saw her.

She stood at a juncture console, staring at the

readout screen there, trying to make sense of the symbols on the screen. They were in Heveian, my native language, but little did she know there was a setting that easily switched the words over to the common galactic tongue. But she probably couldn't read that either. Not all humans knew it, even now.

I crossed my arms, leaned against a metal stanchion, and watched. She muttered to herself, shaking her head in annoyance.

I should've been furious. At least annoyed, but her confusion was so obvious, I found myself grinning instead. This was entertaining—a human wandering these areas with no idea what she was looking at. She couldn't access anything, through the console, at least. She didn't have an authorization code and *that* was what the screen was demanding. She'd apparently tried to do something on it, and she was thwarted by the login prompt.

At last, she turned around. She saw me standing there and her eyes went wide. She clapped a hand to her chest, and a surprised little *oh!* popped out of her.

"Can I help you with something?" I drawled.

She stared at me for a moment, unable to find words, which was even cuter. "What are you doing here?" she finally asked.

I laughed at her audacity. "You know this is *my* ship, don't you? I'm allowed to go anywhere I want. You, on the other hand, are not."

"I didn't know there are restrictions on where I'm allowed to go," she said.

I spread my arms. "The maintenance and engineering areas weren't on the tour." I shook my head. "You can't come back here. You could break something."

She regarded me for a moment. She wore a slim-fitting black outfit that went from just under her chin to her feet. "I just wanted to see how things work," she said, going for a different approach. "I've never been on a ship like this."

"You could learn all about it from Hoc, if you would speak to him. Or the ship interface can offer information, too."

"Forgive me, but I have little trust in robots."

"They're cybots," I corrected. "And I'm sure they're very different from the way they were fifty-two years ago."

She shrugged. "Maybe. But one was hacked once, when I was working on a job, and it caused a lot of trouble." She shook her head. "They're just not safe. Anyone can break into them."

"Not Hoc. He has his own mind about things."

"And that doesn't concern you at all?" Dark splotches appeared on her cheeks. "I'm sorry, one of the things my employers worried about was artificial intelligence taking over and destroying us."

I sighed. "You have a lot to learn about the time you are currently living in, but it won't happen down here. And it's far too cold for you here." I swept my hand back towards the way we came. "I will lead you back to the common area of the ship and ask you not to come back here again."

She didn't move. She crossed her arms and cocked her head, shivering from the cold, which her clothing did nothing to protect her from. "How *did* you find me back here?"

"I have my ways." There was no chance I was telling her that I had sensors set up through the entire engineering and power control system of the ship. If I did, she would find a way to disable them. I stepped close, crowding her a little. "I told you. I know every inch of this ship and it's my job to keep unauthorized persons out of sensitive areas."

"So this is a sensitive area?"

My gaze slid over her, taking in the defiance. "What are you looking for?" I asked softly.

I saw her throat work as she swallowed heavily. "I want to find a way off this ship."

"Impossible," I said. "There's nowhere to go."

Her eyes flashed. "I will find a way off the ship if it kills me."

I didn't like the edge of truth I heard in those words. I stepped closer, planting my hands on either side of her shoulders as she pressed her back up against a metal tube casing. "Why?"

She shook her head. "I won't be brainwashed like those other women. I won't just stay here and be somebody's...wife? Mistress? Whatever they are, I won't be one."

I snorted out a laugh. "Do you find it so inconceivable that Kora and Harp fell in love with the likes of us?" I tilted my head and leaned in towards her ear. "Are we that hideous to you?" I enjoyed the shiver that went through her, which had nothing to do with the cold. I could see her pulse fluttering in her throat. Her tongue came out to wet her lips.

Her gaze moved over me, slowly, reluctantly, and her nostrils flared. "It's not about what you look like," she said. "But who has the power here."

"Not one female here lacks power," I said. "They can leave, if they want. And we would lay down our lives to protect them."

Our gazes locked. A fascinating sort of tension crackled between us. Her chest rose and fell with the same flutter as her pulse. Her eyes darkened. A slender, but very capable, hand came to rest on my chest. My muscles jumped at the contact. "You see?" I asked softly. "I am just as affected by you, as you are by me. Perhaps *you* are the ones brainwashing us."

Her lips parted and her brows furrowed, as if considering that point. "What *is* this?" she whispered.

I shrugged one shoulder and experimentally placed a hand on her hip. "Attraction," I said, simply. "Our bodies are telling us something but our brains are too stubborn to listen."

"No," she said roughly. "The brain is too smart to listen to the body's nonsense." The hand on my chest pushed and I stepped away easily, offering no resistance.

She slid past me, but I grabbed her arm before she

was out of reach. Her gaze snapped to mine, hot and fiery and *there*—attraction was a flame in those dark depths. She felt it just like I did, perhaps even more so.

I let my thumb slide over her upper arm. I could feel the silk of her skin through the thin layer of fabric. I shook my head slowly. "Don't let me catch you in here again," I said, in a growl that was the result of acute arousal. My cock was a thick, aching rod in my pants. My gums were sore where my fangs had lengthened.

Her chin tipped up defiantly. "Or what?"

I looked down at her, my little fighter. "I am responsible for the functioning of this ship and the lives on it," I said. "Don't test me, little female." With that, I brushed past her, exiting before her in what I considered a strong, if somewhat dramatic, exit. It allowed her the chance to find her own way out and think about what I'd said.

And, of course, I monitored her progress as she made her way out to the normal part of the ship. I went to my room, which doubled as my workroom, and set to work at adding more security to the hatches. This female was a challenge. Fortunately, I liked challenges.

CHAPTER 7

Dani

Okay, yes. It shook me up to be caught like that by Wulfrex. I needed to find out how he knew I was there. The obvious explanation was the vitals sensor on my wrist.

That thing needed to go. That was my first order of business. It was careless of me to go into those passageways with it on. I hurried back to the room I shared with Arria, hoping she wouldn't be in there. She wasn't. That meant I could work this sensor bracelet off my wrist without an audience.

I took out the blunt, butter knife I had stowed in a pocket and began scratching at the surface, trying to find a seam. There *had* to be one. It went on my wrist somehow. It had to come off.

As I worked, I thought about the tech I had seen in the underbelly of the cruiser. It was beyond anything I could've imagined. I'd thought I knew what high-tech was.

I didn't. Alien technology was so far beyond anything we had on Earth at the time when I was there, and the implications were mind-boggling. The fuel they used was nothing like what we'd had. I learned enough from the computer interface in the room to know that this cruiser ran on a power-rich crystal source called *vistran*. It had to be the same that the UCP wanted to extract from the Heveians' home planet.

It was an incredible power source, according to what I read. It burned clean, lasted an unbelievably long time, and when harnessed properly, was extremely stable. It was also extraordinarily rare, which would explain why such lengths were being taken to steal it from the Heveians.

Unfortunately, and I *was* embarrassed to admit it, when I was in the guts of the cruiser, I couldn't make any sense of what I was looking at. It was foreign from any Earth-based systems. But I *would* figure it out. I knew there were shuttles or smaller transports here. I just had to find them, and know how to use them. The latter was the key. No point in stealing a transport ship if I couldn't fly it.

There was a sound at the door. I assumed it was Arria returning from wherever she had been. I quickly set aside the butter knife and acted like I wasn't doing anything.

But when the door opened, it wasn't Arria standing there. It was that robot, or, rather, cybot, Hoc. I tensed up and stared at him as he walked in as smoothly and calmly as if he were a human being.

"Good afternoon, Dani Ling. Jorok received an alert that your vital signs monitoring device was behaving strangely and asked me to check on you."

I bared my teeth in a quick wince. "Nothing is wrong with it," I said coldly. "I was trying to remove it."

Hoc's shiny, brassy head cocked to one side. "Why? Is it causing you pain?"

"It's causing me *stress*." I stuck out my arm towards him. "I don't like being monitored. Can you remove it?"

"Of course, I can," the cybot replied with a touch of reproach. "But Jorok thinks—"

"I don't care what he thinks." I sounded rude and I didn't mean to, but speaking to this entity was unnerving. "Wulfrex said we have freedoms on this ship. If that's true, then I choose to have this removed." I kept my arm sticking out with the bracelet dangling from my wrist.

"Very well." The cybot walked up to me. I felt his metal fingers against my skin as he held the bracelet in two places and squeezed. There, I saw the faintest of seams appear. With a quick flick of his hand, the bracelet separated into two pieces and fell into his hand. "There," he said. "Is that better?"

I nodded. "Thank you."

"Well, there is some progress," he said.

"What's that?"

The black circle in the center of his head was flat and

unchanging, but I could swear there was a hint of hurt in the way he held himself. "You saying *thank you* to a cybot."

I rubbed my now bare wrist. "I'm sorry," I said, shoulders slumping. "I didn't mean to sound rude. But there were no cybots in my time, and the robots were wildly different than anything like you. It's alarming, to be honest." And here I was talking to a cybot like it was a real, living thing.

"I am aware of the state of nonorganic beings from your time. And I understand your apprehension. I assure you, I cannot be hacked and I have no desire— either programmed or of my personal calculations—to harm anyone. Believe it or not, I love the people on the ship."

I jolted at those words. "You *love* them?"

"Consider, for a moment, that perhaps one who knows love is not as primitive or dangerous as you might think. I have nearly been destroyed multiple times to save my crew. And they, believe it or not, have done the same to save me." He paused. "You look confused."

"No, I... Yes. I am." I rubbed my temples. "I'm trying to figure all this out."

"It's difficult for you, a human from a past time, to comprehend that I, a being made of metal and *plastoid*, can feel something like love. It must come naturally to you."

"No. Love does *not* come naturally to me. I've never known it, and I never will." I snapped my mouth shut, shocked that I admitted such a thing out loud.

"Oh," said Hoc, clearly taken aback. "I hope you're wrong about that."

I had nothing to say to that. All I could do was stand there and stare at him.

"I hope you find love one day. It's nourishing to the soul—and yes, I believe I have one." He nodded his shiny head, gave a slight bow, and walked back towards the door. "I believe you have one, too."

With that, he turned and left, leaving me alone with my thoughts, minus a tracking bracelet, but with a whole lot more to consider. I could read the subtext of what he was saying. How evolved was I if I didn't have the basic connections that made a human a person?

I scrubbed my fingers through my hair and forced my mind back to the problem at hand. If I didn't find a shuttle, or wrest control of this ship before Claire Turich awakened and recognized me as the one who killed her partner, it wouldn't matter how much love I did or didn't know. I would be the villain. Or, rather, they would *know* I was the villain.

This wasn't the first time I had given serious thought to the course of my life. Typically, assassins like myself didn't live terribly long. I doubted my handlers expected to still be handling me when I turned thirty. I had a knack of squirming out of tight spots, which had made me slightly famous in the dark little corner of the world where I'd existed.

But now, hearing a cybot, of all things, remind me of

what I was missing, made my throat tighten uncomfort-ably. I sat down in one of the seats and asked the inter-face screen to show me what it could on the current state of Earth's politics.

The computer offered me recaps of each five-year block I'd missed, with the highlights of each one. It showed how the world had changed since humans had gained access to farther points in the galaxy, and influ-ence from our knowledge of physics and biology had blown up and changed.

Somehow, some things had not. There were still various differing points of view, disputes over land and ideologies, and problems, which I had hoped would be resolved by now but persisted, like hunger and homelessness. There was less of those things, but it was still a problem on Earth, even now. Fortunately, there were a lot more options for humans. People were leaving for other parts of the galaxy, for space stations, lunar stations, and even an impressive colony on Mars.

I looked up as Arria walked in. She was wrapped in a robe and wet, presumably from the pool. "Hello." I greeted her with a smile and gestured to the screen. "I'm catching up on what I missed."

Arria flopped in the seat beside me, winding her long hair on the top of her head and tying the whole thing in a knot. "That's a lot. How are you managing it?"

"I don't know yet," I replied with a slightly deranged-sounding laugh. "So, the way you grew up, you were insulated from all the stuff going on in the world. That must've been strange."

"I didn't know any better," she said. "When we saw ships flying overhead, some enormous ones, we were told that they were evil and to look away." She shook her head with a rueful smile. "So, yes, I suppose strange is a good word for it."

"Not as strange as being frozen for fifty-two years and waking up to *this*." I spread my arms, encompassing the ship, the Heveians, everything.

"That's true," said Arria. "You would be in your eighties right now had you not been cryogenically frozen." She shook her head. "Here's an interesting question: Do you count your age by when you were frozen, or your true chronological age?"

"Well, I feel pretty good for eighty-two. Does that count for something?"

"We'll stick with thirty as your age, then." She turned those keen eyes on me. "Do you have *any* memory of being abducted?"

I frowned and thought about what I *did* remember. It wasn't a lot. "I was at a luxury hotel. I was there to see someone speak and give a presentation. After that, I... did the job I was there to do, and then—" I shook my head. "There was a flash of light and nothing until I woke up a couple days ago on this ship. I have a really good memory, usually. Bothers me I can't remember more."

"You remember more than what the rest of us do. Maybe something will come back to you."

"I hope so. Although, sometimes, it's better to not remember."

"It'll be okay," Arria said in her gentle voice. "I promise."

I shook my head sadly, but didn't argue. I *wanted* to believe her. We spent the rest of the day chatting and just hanging out, like two girlfriends would. At dinner-time, Harp and Kora came in. They got food from the dispenser and sat down in chairs and we all ate together as if this was a perfectly normal thing to do.

But it wasn't, for me. I watched with curious interest as conversations flowed, along with wine and food that I couldn't eat, since I was still on a restricted diet.

Kora told a funny story about Ryland mistaking her scented body oil for his sore muscle oil, and how he spent the whole day smelling like lilacs.

"And I didn't even have the heart to tell him," said Kora. "He smelled so nice."

"Did anyone else notice?" asked Harp.

"They must've," said Kora. "I mean, he doesn't *usually* smell like a bouquet of flowers, does he?"

Harp let out a hoot of laughter. "They smell good, but not like flowers."

"How did *he* not smell it?" asked Arria.

Kora rolled her eyes. "Who knows? He's used to smelling flowers since he lives with me. Our room smells like it. *I* smell like it. He must not have noticed."

There were a few chuckles, then the chatter moved to the woman who was stubbornly remaining unconscious.

I kept quiet during this, not having anything helpful to add. They moved on from this, too. I began to relax with these women, who were so comfortable together, and who deftly included me in their conversations.

"What's your favorite flavor of ice cream?" Harp asked. She had gone to the dispenser and was punching something in.

I thought back, trying to remember if I even *had* a favorite flavor of ice cream. "Peanut butter chocolate," I said. The memory of it made my mouth water. "But it's not going to let me eat it."

Harp glanced at me with a sly look. "It will if it doesn't know it's for you."

I grinned back at her. "I'll blame you if I spend half the night in the bathroom."

"You won't." She turned back to the machine. "This thing actually makes really good ice cream. Peanut butter chocolate is one we already have loaded in, so good choice." She gave me a wink and began to unload glass bowls of ice cream.

Kora got mint chip, Arria chose half pistachio and half chocolate fudge, and Harp went with maple walnut. She handed me the generous bowl of chocolate peanut butter with a smile. "We're working on the right consistency of hot fudge, but it's not there yet. Still kind of grainy and it turns rubbery when it hits the ice cream."

I picked up the spoon that was already in the bowl, scooped off a little bit and put it between my lips. "This is...*amazing*. Thank you." I moaned. "Oh my god. So good."

"Right?" Kora gently tapped my knee as she nodded. "It's delicious. And it's better for you than Earth ice cream. No dairy."

"How can this taste so good without dairy?" I asked around the giant spoonful in my mouth.

"The wonders of alien technology," Harp said, with a flourishing hand.

After ice cream, glasses of wine were passed out—another miraculous production from the machine on the wall. And the talking continued. By the time Kora and Harp left, I was relaxed. My face was slightly sore from so much laughing and smiling. My chest had a light ache in it from, ironically, how much pleasure I just had talking with women. It was a longing for this to be part of my life for real.

But as I crawled into bed that night and lay in the darkened room, listening to Arria's soft breathing, I reminded myself that this was *not* my home and these women were not my friends. In another world, in a different version of reality, I could laugh with them without any worries.

But in *this* reality, I did not have such a luxury.

CHAPTER 8

Dani

S trictly speaking, I *didn't* go back into the passageways Wulfrex had warned me about.

I went to a different passageway. One that led through some ductwork and into the hangar that held transport vehicles. I had a hard time finding it. No doubt Wulfrex had tinkered with the schematics I had access to, but I had an idea where it was from when I had full access.

Once I figured out the layout of the ship, I was able to discern where the hangar was, and how to get into it without going through the main door. That, I tried, and it was definitely locked. Honestly, I would have been disappointed if Wulfrex *hadn't* restricted my access, but it was annoying to have to take the long way in. And I'm not going to say I didn't make a few wrong turns. At one point, I found myself at the waste disposal area, and they don't smell better on fancy alien ships than they do on Earth.

The hangar was darkened as the only lights were the pale dim circles glowing on the floor beneath each small aircraft. I counted six. They were all a little different, apparently sourced—stolen or purchased—from different places. One ship was partially dismantled and sat there like a dejected, broken toy.

I went to the closest one, which sat there with its side hatch wide open, almost beckoning me to go in and take it. When I entered the small ship, I knew I wouldn't be able to do anything with it. There was no cockpit, or operator interface, or whatever they called it on these kinds of ships. I sat in the smooth, sleek chair, which was positioned behind a smooth metal plate with no instruments. *Nothing.* Not even a button. No wonder the door was open. Only someone who knew the secrets of this particular shuttle could operate it.

I left, chagrined, because that chair was comfortable. The next ship was locked up tight. I couldn't even find the door. It was seamless against the hull of the ship. The third one was normal enough. I managed to pry open the hatch and climb inside. It was pretty small, but that didn't matter. It was only me and I didn't have cargo. This one had a chair with a flat-screen instrument panel. It looked confusing, but not insurmountably so. I had figured out plenty of things. I would figure out this.

I reached for a large, flat green button. If the basics were at least similar to the way ships were on Earth, I could—

"I would not press that, if I were you."

My head whipped around at the sound of that deep husky voice. "You," I hissed.

He was standing there, leaning against the wall in the exact same pose as when he caught me in the ship maintenance passageways. He wore one of those clear chest pieces he seemed so fond of, that showed the chiseled planes of his chest and abdomen to perfection. His arms were bare and on his legs he wore a pair of pants with far too many pockets and pouches. He spread his hands. "Here to stop you from doing something you'll regret."

I surged to my feet. "You have no idea what I regret."

"Oh, I think I do."

"Yes," I said. "I regret every decision I made that landed me on this ship." I slashed my hand through the air. "Because just about anywhere else is better than being here, with you."

The annoying male grinned at me. "Oh, please. You adore me."

I snorted out a disbelieving laugh. "I do not. My feelings for you are quite the opposite of adoration."

He pushed away from the wall and came closer. "You're just afraid to admit your true feelings."

He was teasing me. Outrageously, blatantly, teasing me. And as infuriating as it was, it was also…exciting. Intriguing. "How did you find me this time?" I held up my wrist that no longer had a bracelet. "Did Jorok implant something in me?"

"On the contrary," said Wulfrex. "Jorok removed a tracking implant from you. You had something imbedded just here." He pressed a calloused finger between my breasts. Heat curled out from his touch.

"That's not true," I breathed.

"It is," he said lightly, retracting that finger. "Back on Earth, someone knew your position all the time. Jorok removed it. He didn't put a new one in."

"Then how did you—?"

"Dani, this is my hangar," he said. "This is my ship. If I am not aware that someone is lurking around, then I am not doing my job."

"You didn't answer my question."

He leaned even closer and I picked up his pleasant, masculine scent, the sharp flash of his eyes, and the curl of his lips. "And I'm not going to," he said silkily.

That just annoyed me more. "Wulfrex, I just want to get off the ship."

"Why?" he asked, crossing his arms.

"None of your business *why*. I just need to." I looked around with a flicker of desperation that I knew was showing in the tightness of my jaw and the strain around my eyes.

"If you tell me why, I might help you."

My shoulders dropped. "I can't tell you. It's...not good."

I said that last bit looking down and away from him. I was running out of fight. Running out of options. Wherever I went, Wulfrex was there. I might as well just turn myself in and deal with the brig.

He tipped my chin up with one finger. "Dani, you're talking to a space pirate. I'm not going to hold anything you say against you."

I held his gaze. "Yes, you would. *I* would. Those three other women? They will. I didn't lead a normal life, you know."

"I figured that out when Jorok told me he dug a tracking chip out of your breast bone." He reached out, took my hand and tugged me towards him.

I didn't, *couldn't* resist. My feet moved forward and I stood in front of him, feeling uncertain and vulnerable. "I'm sorry, Wulfrex," I said in a whisper. "I just can't talk about it."

"Yet."

I said nothing, locked there, frozen in an embrace that was coming, but not quite there yet. His magnetism was so strong, I couldn't have pulled myself away if I wanted to. And I didn't want to.

He cupped a hand behind my neck. His grip could have encircled my entire throat, but he held me there in a gentle, featherlight hold. "It appears we are at an impasse, then," he said.

I opened my mouth to say something, but no words came. I just stood there, so close, gazing at him.

There was a gentle pressure on my neck as he tugged closer. Did I resist like I should have? No, I let myself be pulled in. I stood still, breathless and hungry, as he lowered his head.

I closed my eyes and leaned up as his mouth came down on mine. Firm, expert lips moved over mine, claiming my mouth. It felt like something inevitable. Like I had come here expecting, or at least hoping, that he'd find me and do exactly this. He leaned in on a groan, as if it had been his plan all along to kiss me senseless. Maybe it was.

Either way, I had no defense against this—this madness. This complete evacuation of my good senses. The abandonment of my *training*. Good god, my training was useless now. This male wiped away every useful skill I thought I had stitched into my very being.

Nope. Here I was, turning to mush in the arms of an alien male I barely knew. And I couldn't bring myself to get it together and push him away, yet.

Just a little longer, then I'd stop him. I'd—I'd…oh, fuck it. I wrapped my arms around his thick neck and kissed him back for all I was worth.

He pressed up against me. The whole long, solid length of him, including the hard rod of his cock on my belly. It wouldn't take much for him to just take me here. Long blue hair ran like thick silk through my fingers. It would be so easy…

The tips of his fangs brushed against my lip with a prick of pain. His eyeteeth seemed sharper and longer than what I remembered. Despite the gentle caress of his tongue and lips, my body tensed up. I wriggled away from him as much as I could in the tight space, my eyes wide with surprise.

"No," I said.

He went still, but did not back away. "What's

wrong?" he asked in a low voice brimming with hunger and rough with arousal.

All the reasons why I was in this hangar in the first place roared to the forefront of my mind. "I-I can't," I stammered. "This isn't right."

He eased back a little, but his fingers slid down my cheek in a silken caress. I could see those long fangs now, so much longer than they were before.

I shook my head, remembering that he was of an alien species I knew little about. They were vampires, it appeared. I could still taste my own blood on my tongue. He looked like he wanted to sink his teeth right into me.

My hand went to my pocket where I had stowed a fork and a blunt butter knife from my room. I had to pick one. My hand curled around the knife. It was thicker. It had a better chance of getting through whatever his chest piece was made of. "Are you going to bite me?" I asked nervously.

He grinned wide, showing *all* those teeth. "Oh, yes, little human. But I promise you will enjoy it."

That was all I needed to hear. I did not want to become a vampire, or be bitten by a vampire, or have my blood drained, no matter how much he might think I'd "enjoy it."

Instincts kicked in. Training rushed back to my mind. My heart hammered like mad in my chest. "You won't drink my blood today," I cried, and thrust forward with the butter knife. It sank into his abdomen.

CHAPTER 9

Wulfrex

looked down and saw one of the eating utensils that must've come from her room stuck in the *plastoid* shell of my chest piece. The tip of it had gotten through and a tiny drop of blue blood oozed from the nick it produced.

This was my casual body armor, which I wore when working, to avoid hurting myself. It happened often enough when working in dark places with lots of pointed metal, superheated fluids, and caustic chemicals. I often wore a helmet, too. Perhaps that would have been helpful in this case. "Why did you do that?" I asked, offended.

She had edged away from me, slightly crouched, with the look of a feral animal. "You just said you were going to bite me." She pointed at my mouth. "You *did bite me, a little." She looked at the knife stuck in my armor. "What *is* that stuff made out of?"

I yanked the knife out of my chest piece and stuck it in a pouch of my pants that also held a collection of random connectors and parts that I always thought I'd need, but rarely did. "That's not important right now," I said. "You *stabbed* me." I looked down at the tiny cut on my abdomen, and then up at her. "I'm bleeding."

"Oh, stop it," she said. "It's barely a scratch."

"That's not the point," I said. "You. Stabbed me."

"Yeah," she said, slowly, as if speaking to a child. "You said you were going to bite me."

"That's what Heveians do with their mates," I said, with the daunting realization that Dani would have no clue whatsoever about what my species did during rutting, sometimes. I groaned and rubbed a hand over my face. "Ah, fuck," I said. "You had no idea. I'm sorry."

"I didn't know you were vampires." She crossed her arms tightly over her chest and took a tiny step towards the exit. "I'd rather keep my blood in my veins, thank you very much."

I shook my head, cursing myself. "The other women did not talk to you about this?"

"About what?" she asked. "That their brave, handsome rescuers drink their blood? No, they missed that part."

"We don't drink blood," I said, disgusted. I remembered Ryland mentioning that Kora had the same fear in the beginning. "I don't know what creatures you have on your planet that drink the blood of your females, but we do no such thing." I ran my tongue over my long fangs. They were slowly thickening and retracting to their typical length.

"Then what do you do?" She peered at me warily, having removed another utensil from her pocket. This one was a fork. She waved it in the direction of my mouth. "You just bite women for the fun of it?"

"Yes," I said. "I mean, *no*." Sweet stars, this was getting more complicated by the moment. "Our fangs take in a small amount of blood from our mates when we rut with them. It enters our bloodstream, and our saliva brings tremendous pleasure to our mates," I explained. That was the most efficient version I could come up with on the spot. Hopefully it would alleviate her worries that I had intentions of ripping open her throat and—ew—drinking her blood. "If it's any consolation, I've never wanted to bite a female before."

She didn't even blink. "What a deep honor you bestow upon me," she said. "But I must decline." Sarcasm dripped from her words.

"Don't worry." I showed her my teeth. "The urge has definitely passed, and I will not kiss you again."

"You better not. If you try, I'll be ready with something sharper." She brandished that fork again and I resisted the urge to pluck it from her fingers.

"So will I," I growled. Desire still pumped fast and hot through my veins. My cock was still hard and eager to rut. I glowered at her, more aroused than I'd ever been. "I am warning you now, Dani. Stay out of the hangars. Stay out of the mechanical areas of this ship. Do not cause any more trouble here." I narrowed my eyes. I did not find this amusing any longer. "We will return you to Earth at our earliest convenience. Until then, you will have to endure life on this cruiser. I don't care what your secrets are. I don't care what your reasons are for wanting to get off of this ship so badly that you would attempt to steal our property and *stab* me, but this nonsense ends now."

She glared up at me with the hateful restraint of one who knows they have no leverage. With slow movements, she nodded, tucked the fork back in her pocket, and slipped out of the shuttle.

I moved to the hatch and watched her as she walked, stiffed-backed, to the exit and out. The door slid shut behind her. I sagged against the arched opening of the hatch, resting my back against one side and propping up a foot on the other. My hand moved to my crotch and idly rubbed my cock through my pants.

I wanted to rut with her until she screamed my name and, yes, I wanted to bite her. I had said the word mate casually, but it was no casual term. Heveians often recognized their mates because of the often overwhelming desire to bite them, to share blood with them. It was the most intimate act my species performed. It was no small matter.

And it massively complicated things.

CHAPTER 10

Wulfrex

The first thing I did after changing my chest piece and cleaning up that small cut on my stomach, was to lock down all sectors of the ship. I gathered my small engineering crew in the tiny, private control room that held a centralized console for the primary power systems of the ship.

They grumbled at the extra security. They would have to perform extra steps to do basic maintenance now. What was the reason for it, they wanted to know.

I told them that one of the new females had extraordinary curiosity and had not yet learned the rules, and that until she did, these measures needed to be taken. I didn't tell them or anyone else about her stabbing me. I didn't see how that would be helpful, and besides, it still smarted that the audacious female had managed to injure me at all.

I also further restricted Dani's access to schematics and information, shutting down all but the bare basics to Dani in her room that she shared with Arria.

Arria had a small, handheld screen that was all but adhered to her at all times. She read on it constantly and that device remained as it was. It was just the large screen in their shared room that was essentially useless now.

I had to brief Ryland and Axlos on the security measures. On the main deck, I stood with them around our central screen, which was our unofficial meeting location for all discussions.

"Do you see her as a security threat?" Ryland asked directly.

"I see her as a resourceful, if terrified, human who has some business on Earth that she regards as life-and-death." I rolled my shoulders. "I've locked down certain areas of the ship in case she tries a stunt again. I don't believe she will."

Ryland nodded to Hoc, who sat at a console pod with a cable attached to a port in his chest.

He looked over and disconnected the cable. "Yes, Ryland?"

"Can you please bring Dani here?" he asked. "I need to speak with her immediately."

"Yes, of course." The cybot rose and left the deck.

My stomach dropped. If Dani didn't watch herself during this conversation, she would end up in the brig, which was not a pleasant place. There were two cells, a small one for beings her size, and a larger one. She would be put in the smaller one. It was four walls, a ceiling and a floor of cold, hard metal and nothing else. We had not dedicated much in the way of conveniences or comforts to our brig.

Axlos turned to me. "What is your association with this female?"

I sighed. "I want her," I replied honestly. "I want to rut with her and bite her." I waved my hand around in an effort to find the words I was looking for. "Everything just lights up when she's around. I don't understand this feeling."

Ryland looked pained. "I understand the feeling."

Axlos turned his gaze to the ceiling. "Stars, Wulfrex," he said. "You know how to pick them."

He would know, having been my friend for the whole of my life. The females of my past tended to be wild and fun and vaguely terrifying. Dani had the vaguely terrifying part down, at least.

Hoc returned with a stiff-looking Dani by his side. "Do you want to see me?" she asked tightly.

Ryland turned to her, arms crossed and a frown on his face. "Wulfrex tells me we have had to increase security by locking down whole sectors of the ship because *you* attempted to steal one of our transports."

Dani had the nerve to look accusatorially at me, as if I should've kept this a secret. She bowed her head. "That's right. It was a mistake. I'm sorry, and I shouldn't have done it."

I resisted the urge to roll my eyes. That was an obligatory apology if I ever heard one.

Ryland's expression didn't change. "Look. As soon as we complete our missions here, we can discuss returning you to Earth, but until then, we cannot."

"Yes, sir," she said.

"Furthermore, those transport ships are our property. We rightfully stole them from freighters that we *risked our lives* to raid, and they are an important part of our fleet."

She pressed her lips together and blinked. No one else seemed to realize that she was trying very hard not to laugh at that. "I didn't realize that, sir," she choked out contritely.

"As the security officer on the ship, I'm telling you now—one more infraction and you will be spending the remainder of your time in the brig." Ryland was on a roll now. He had on his most authoritative face. He looked like a teacher scolding a youngling in the schoolyard.

Dani nodded. "I understand, sir."

Ryland growled. "Will you stop calling me *sir*? You are not my subordinate."

She looked up at him, then turned her gaze to me. "I'm truly sorry." Her gaze dropped to my abdomen, then flicked back up to my eyes. "For everything. I should not have done that."

I inclined my head towards her. "Apology accepted. Now, no more—"

I was cut off by an alert, and Drave, who had been at his console blissfully ignoring us, pulled off his headpiece.

He turned towards us. "Hate to interrupt, but our scanning probes came back with something."

All attention was on him. Drave had missed what we were talking about, so he launched into the probe's findings without notice of Dani's presence. "The likely location of our missing Heveian male has been determined. There is an abandoned mining operation on an ice moon of a planetary system not far from here. Only, it does not appear to be abandoned any longer. Multiple heat signatures and active exhaust vents are present, as well as machinery needed to enable life support under the surface of this moon. I've deployed further detail-scanning probes to determine the ideal entry point, and to scan the underground system." He raised a brow. "Shall I begin to organize a shuttle party?"

Ryland turned to me, glancing quickly at Dani. "I need Hoc here. Can you take our guest back to her quarters?"

"Happily," I said. I ushered Dani back towards the door and out of the main deck.

She looked at me in the hallway. "You know, this could be a trap. Your enemies could be luring you there."

"What *are* you?" I frowned down at her. "You're a spy, or something like that, aren't you?"

"Hmm." She rolled her shoulders. "Something like that."

CHAPTER 11

Dani

Wulfrex left me at my quarters, but I didn't stay there. No, I didn't go someplace I wasn't allowed. I went to the medical lab where Dr. Claire Turich still lay motionless. I sat on the bed beside her, the one that used to be mine. I gazed down at her sleeping form, feeling resigned and just tired.

"Who knew you would cause me so much trouble?" I murmured to myself.

If she opened her eyes right now, what would she do? Scream? Hide in fear? Either of those would be reasonable reactions, considering what I did the last time she saw me.

"Come to check on our patient?" asked Jorok as he entered the room.

I looked up. "How is she doing?"

He shrugged. "I'm seeing improvements in brain function. She's just taking longer than you did to come out of it."

I nodded. "Any idea when she might wake up?"

Jorok sat down at his desk, if you would call it that. It was more like an L-shaped table, crowded with devices and screens. "She could wake up during this conversation. She could wake up next week. Or a month from now. It really depends on her."

I kept a neutral expression on my face, but my chest tightened. She could wake up at any moment. And then my role in ending the life of a great scientific mind would be exposed.

Jorok looked over at me with one raised blue eyebrow. "Hear you have been in a bit of trouble."

I shrugged one shoulder. "I may have been poking around in places I shouldn't have."

"You're very eager to get off the ship." Jorok folded his hands on his lap and faced me, therapist style. "Is there anything you want to talk about?"

I thought about telling him. I really did think about it. On Earth, doctors weren't allowed to share with anyone what their patients told them, unless there was some legal reason. But this wasn't Earth. Instead, because my mind was so conflicted, I leaned forward, rested my elbows on my knees and dropped my head in my hands. "I did some things fifty-two years ago that I'm not proud of. I guess you could say they're haunting me now."

He nodded. "All of us here have a list of things we

THE ALIEN'S BLADE   89

wish we could take back. I guess you could say you haven't really lived if you have no regrets."

A harsh laugh gurgled from my lips. "Well, then, I certainly have lived a very full life." I rose. "Are you going on the mission to that moon?"

"You know about that, do you?" He shook his head with a smile. "I would like to, but I need to be here if she wakes up. Like you, her vital signs need to be monitored after she comes out of the hibernation." His gaze dropped to my wrist. "You could've asked me. I would've removed that for you."

I felt some heat in my cheeks. "Hoc did it for me."

"After you tried to pry it off yourself." He held up a hand as I opened my mouth to speak. "It's fine. I just want you to know that I'm here to help."

I nodded again, feeling heavier and more weary of it all. "You know, it would be a whole lot easier if you guys were all assholes," I said.

"Easier for what? To hate us?" He gave me a crooked grin. "At one time we were. Hence the regrets. But when your species is facing genocide in the form of a deadly disease, it reframes your perspective."

"I can see how that would be."

He gestured to Claire. "I'll let you know when she wakes up," he said. There was a knowing look in his eyes. I could imagine it wasn't much of a secret that I knew who this woman was. But Jorok didn't push me. He wasn't trying to force a confession.

"Thanks," I said, and ducked out of his lab.

I went back to my room and lay down in my bed.

When the other women came, I stayed there and said I was tired and not hungry. They tucked me in—*actually tucked me in*—with my blanket and left a cup of tea on the table beside my bed, before assembling in the seating area with their meals.

I pretended to be asleep, but I listened. They talked about the rescue mission the males were going on, which was what I wanted to hear about. It was scheduled for three days' time. Ryland, Wulfrex, and Axlos were going. Drave and Jorok were staying on the ship.

My brain worked like mad as I lay there. If I was going to get away from this place, this was my chance. Probably the only one. All I needed to do was sneak onto that transport, and when they left to enter the mine, take off with it. I felt bad about stranding them on the surface, but it would only be temporary. They had other transports, and the whole cruiser. A new shuttle would quickly be sent down to pick them up. I wouldn't be leaving anyone to die.

And I had three days to plan. I could make this happen.

I kept my nose clean for those three days. I didn't go anywhere I wasn't supposed to—not that I could, with the most interesting parts of the ship locked down. For the most part, I kept out of everyone's way. I did all the right things. I swam in the pool that everyone raved about. It *was* actually really nice. I exercised. I ate. I smiled and said hello to everyone. I made myself a few things from the replicator. I gave the appearance that I was settling in and accepting my place here. I was *sociable*. I thought I had everyone fooled. I didn't.

Wulfrex wasn't buying it. I had also managed to give him a wide berth, but when we did cross paths, he would look at me like he expected me to do something awful at any moment. I would return these suspicious looks with the most innocent expression I could conjure. When I saw him, I wasn't friendly, but polite. I did not seek him out. And he did not seek me out.

It was the morning of the third day. The ship was in a bit of a bustle because the shuttle party was leaving that evening. I was returning from the pool in my bathing suit and robe, just walking down the corridor towards my room. I was thinking about the plan I had devised and not paying attention to the footsteps behind me.

Suddenly Wulfrex was there, towering, looming like a huge, silver, blue-haired bear. His slitted, catlike eyes narrowed on me as he fell into step beside me. "Don't even think about it," he said.

"Think about what?" I looked up at him with wide eyes.

"Everything will be locked down. I've seen to it personally."

I looked straight ahead. "I don't know what you're talking about."

"If you're thinking of stealing the cruiser when we're away," he said, "you'll be stranding us on that moon."

"I have no intentions of stealing a cruiser," I assured him. "Don't worry."

"When it comes to you, I always worry."

I stopped walking and placed a hand on his forearm. "Wulfrex, just don't get hurt, okay? You may be sure it's not a trap, but I'm not."

His brows drew together. "Is that concern I hear in your voice?"

"Would that be so strange?" I asked. "Everyone on this ship has treated me with nothing but kindness. I'm not sure I deserve any of it." I looked down, because every word I was saying was true. None of it was an act. And none of those words were part of the plan. I withdrew my hand from his arm and looked away. "Yeah, I'm concerned. I want to see you make it back in one piece."

We stood there in a strange, awkwardly charged silence. "We'll be fine," he said at last, gruffly.

"Good," I said, and began to walk again.

His big hand wrapped around my forearm and gently stopped me. "Dani, I mean it. Drave and Jorok will be here, and they will put you in the brig if you try anything funny. And our brig is awful. It's noisy, cold, and small. You won't like it."

"I'll keep that in mind, but seriously, you don't need to worry about me."

His thumb slid over my skin and I could not stifle the shiver that went through me. He saw it. His eyes darkened to glittering slits. "Be here when I get back," he growled.

I wanted to say I would. The urge was so strong, I bit my lip to keep from whimpering "okay." Instead, I leaned up on my toes and pressed a fast, hard kiss to his mouth.

He groaned and kissed me back, hungry and raw. With a growl of frustration, he leaned back. "We'll continue this later."

My face was hot and my lips throbbed from his kiss. I knew I was flushed, partly with guilt and partly with the heat of arousal. It made everything sensitive, and everything hungry. I slipped inside my room, closed the door and leaned against it with a sigh.

For a moment, a wild thought crossed my mind of standing there as he returned, battle-weary and dirty, but hot as fuck. And me, leaping into his arms to feel the rush that I always felt around him and relief that he was back safe. I *wanted* that.

I bit back the wave of regret, knowing I couldn't have it. Knowing that I wasn't that woman. The knowledge of that was bitter in my mouth. That kiss was the best I could do. Little did he know, that was my goodbye.

CHAPTER 12

Wulfrex

The smallest of the shuttle transports was a stealth vehicle. It was one of the more high-tech and advanced models that we had stolen, and it flew like a dream. It was also very challenging to operate, as its origin was with a rare species who didn't build it in compliance with the galactic standard.

There was another reason I had chosen *this* shuttle and it was, simply, that Dani couldn't operate it. It had taken *me* weeks to learn how to fly it and I suspected I hadn't yet learned the full extent of its capabilities. My gut told me that Dani would still try to escape the cruiser and could try to sneak aboard the one we were taking. I did not know what she planned to do, but I had to be prepared for all options with her.

I had programed an auto-return sequence into the shuttle, so in the event that *I* could not pilot us home,

Axlos or Ryland could simply activate the controls and it would return them to the cruiser. Dani could try to take it, but the fancy little shuttle wouldn't recognize her as an authorized operator and would lock down, locking *her* inside. She'd be safe and I wouldn't have to worry about her.

Supplies were loaded onto the transport. We didn't know what state the Heveian male would be in when we rescued him, or if there would be more Heveians to rescue, or if we would be taking prisoners, or even some valuable cargo. Weaponry and medical supplies were loaded into the back of the ship. It was one open space and the cargo went in the back.

We filed onto the small transport in full battle armor. The body piece was transparent, reinforced *plastoid* that could withstand numerous blaster shots. We wore helmets with visors with displays that detected heat signatures, and lightweight metal leg and arm armor. Thick boots with gravity-stabilizers completed the ensemble. I had my favorite weapon, a gigantic, plasma flare/blaster combo that, thanks to my size and strength, was manageable for me. It was also really fun to use in practice. Not as much fun in reality. But nevertheless, I was prepared.

Axlos and Ryland took places around me as we lifted off and exited the cruiser's hangar. We discussed what the additional scans had revealed about our mission as I piloted the stealth shuttle using hand motions above the smooth surface of the control panel. I had to wear a special eyepiece when using it, because the controls were holographic forms suspended in the air and only visible through a certain light spectrum.

Axlos sat grimly in the seat beside me. His jaw was set. The fine lines around his eyes were tight. "Before we exit, I want our communication links with Drave checked."

"Affirmative," replied Ryland.

"I updated the range on our links," I said. "And increased penetration for the underground. Unless someone purposefully runs interference, we should have no problems."

"And if they do," said Axlos, "we have a plan for that."

"We find the Heveian first," said Ryland. "No splitting up." He swung his knowing aqua gaze to me. "No distractions. You see some shiny new tech, you keep walking."

I grinned. "Promise. I just want to get back to the cruiser."

"Shocking," Ryland drawled. "You really are attracted to her, aren't you?"

"I am," I said, not bothering to pretend I didn't know who he was talking about. "Against my better judgment, she intrigues me."

"Intrigue isn't all you're feeling," said Axlos. "You said yourself you wanted to—"

I cut him off with a raised hand. "I don't want to think about this when embarking on a mission," I said. "Yes. When we get back to the cruiser, I intend to tell her how I feel and rut with her until she forgets her own name."

Ryland let out a laugh. "If she'll have you."

"She will," I said.

"You're confident," said Ryland. "Sounds like good motivation to get back in one piece."

"It is."

We spent the rest of the short trip to the icy moon discussing the layout of the mine and potential obstacles we might face. We all expected it to be guarded in some way, either by automatic weaponry, living guards, or cybot guards. There would be defenses. No one installed a facility in the Inrex quadrant unless they were hiding something that was very important to someone.

We approached our destination and fell into silence. With the shuttle in stealth mode, we descended to the coordinates that the probes had indicated. The mine and this moon had once been the location of great activity. This was clear by the large bank of sizable hangars that had been built into the side of a rocky cliff midway down a canyon. It was below the layer of ice, which was thousands of meters thick on the surface.

There were hundreds of landing pads in the abandoned hangars and they were huge to accommodate large transports. We flew into one of them, sliding through the membrane-thin atmosphere barrier, which was still in operation.

"Well, that's some luck," I said. "We'll be able to breathe in here."

"How is that still working?" asked Ryland.

"Mines are typically set up with a geothermic power source," I said. "That way, sabotage and attacks can't disrupt the operation. This one's no different. That membrane will be here for thousands of years, unless their entire infrastructure is destroyed."

"Makes for a built-in power source for someone wanting to take over the mine and use it for something else," said Axlos. "Like imprisoning beings and experimenting on them."

"If that's what happened to our Heveian, yes," I said.

Axlos' jaw was tight. "The Mitran warlord said the male had been *altered*. No one is altered on Heveia."

I nodded. "Usually, these mines are ceased because they have become unstable or their valuables have been mined out. It's an ideal place if you're trying to do something you shouldn't, without anyone noticing."

I kept the shuttle in stealth as I set it down on a landing pad. The hangar, expensive as it was, was completely dark. Heveian eyes can see well in low light, and some in no light. What little I could see through the glass window was a whole lot of dusty nothingness. Abandoned parts were dark shapes on the smooth stone floor. The ceiling above was rough-cut and craggy. Water dripped from fissures in the ceiling, creating big puddles on the slick surface.

"I'm going to have to take it out of stealth in order to turn it off," I said. "Hopefully no one checks in here very often."

"It doesn't look like anyone comes in here," Ryland said. "We did choose the hangar farthest from the entrance." He narrowed his eyes. "Hopefully that was a smart move and we don't have to make a hasty retreat."

"A hasty retreat would be welcome," said Axlos, adjusting his armor and tightening his arm pieces. "I don't want to be here any longer than necessary. Something about this place… I don't like it."

That was not something one generally liked to hear from their leader. Axlos rarely expressed such things. When he did, it put us on higher alert.

"We'll be in and out in an hour, at most," said Ryland.

I powered down the transport, strapped my weapon to my back, and tested the coms. After hearing Drave drily admit that he liked us best alive, and request that we return to the cruiser in that form, we exited the shuttle. Before activating the locking mechanism that only the three of us could override with our biometrics, I looked around the dark, still cabin and hoped it was as empty as it appeared. Then, I closed it and we set off across the massive, empty hangar. Our boots echoed through the empty space, splashing in the puddles. The pale glow of our armor trim illuminated the areas just around us.

"Lights off," Axlos ordered.

We shut off our lights and our eyes adjusted further to the darkness. Our dark sight turned the hangar into a world of blue- and gray-hued emptiness. The shapes of discarded spaceship parts were hulking, moldering mounds. Small alien vermin skittered on tiny, tapping legs just beyond the range of our vision. All the while, my heart beat hard, and not with anticipation of a fight.

I had to agree with Axlos. Something about this place wasn't right. The sooner we got out of here, the better.

CHAPTER 13

Dani

I waited until all was clear and the Heveians had left. The storage crate I'd folded myself into was tight and stifling. Carefully, I lifted the lid and pushed through the piles of medical supplies I had hidden myself under.

I stepped carefully onto the floor, half expecting a million alarms to start ringing, but the shuttle stayed quiet. I took a moment to stretch my cramped limbs. I had curled into the fetal position and stayed there so long my joints were screaming at me. But I knew how to wait and I knew how to endure pain. I took a look around.

Of course, Wulfrex had chosen the shuttle that was impossible to operate. The one with the comfortable chair but no discernible instruments and controls. I went to the front and sat down in the seat. I peered out the curved glass before me to see what was going on out there, but saw nothing but darkness.

I got the sense that the hangar we were in was expansive even without hearing Wulfrex, Axlos, and Ryland talking about it. The only thing I could actually see was the shimmering barrier that held the atmosphere inside the hangar and maintained the temperature.

I had heard everything the three Heveians had said. Through them, I'd learned that the air was breathable and the mine was powered by geothermal energy and the power system wasn't likely to break down anytime soon. If what Ryland had said was true, they would be back in an hour, so I had that long to figure out the ship and get out of here. I sat in the chair and observed the smooth surface in front of me.

Wulfrex had figured this out. *He* knew how to fly it, but I hadn't seen him do it. I rubbed my hands together, starting to feel a chill seep through the whole of the ship. Without the power on, it would get brisk in here. I just started touching things. I ran my hands over the smooth metal. I waved my hands in the air in front of me, hoping to activate something. Suddenly, the lights in the ship turned on. Well, some of them. They looked like auxiliary lights. Pale green, and just enough to chase away the shadows in the shuttle.

"Now we're getting somewhere," I murmured to myself. I changed my hand movements, making them a little more erratic to see what else I could activate on the ship. Perhaps there would be some instructions, or a start-up sequence.

Nothing happened. I poked the metal dash. In frustration, I dropped my fist in the middle of it. That did something. Just, not something *good*.

A blue disc the size of a dinner plate appeared in front of my chair, in the center of the dash. It hovered in the air, a foot from my face. I sat back suddenly, snatching my hands away from the console. I gasped as the blue disc shifted and a form began to rise from it in the shape of an all-too familiar male.

A miniature holographic image of Wulfrex was there, flickering, blue, semitransparent, and smug as ever. Even at only a foot high, I couldn't miss his cocky grin. His image stood there, arms crossed, looking amused and a little vexed.

"I hope you don't see this, Dani," drawled Wulfrex in his deep voice. "But if you are seeing this, then your plan is to steal our transport and fly home." The little image of Wulfrex shook his head at me. "Unfortunately for you, I am changing your plans. I had a feeling you might do this, so to ensure that you are safe, you are presently locked and sealed inside this shuttle. The only thing you can power on is life support, lights, and facilities, until our return," mini Wulfrex said. "Enjoy your stay on this fine vessel. Feel free to enjoy refreshments from the food dispenser, and the facilities are here for you to use. I hope you make yourself at home. It's probably the last time you're going to be comfortable in a while, since when we return from our mission, your new accommodations will be in our lovely brig." He smiled charmingly and gave a mock bow. "Stay out of trouble, Dani," he said, and the hologram flickered out.

I sank back in the seat as I let loose a steady stream of curses. *Asshole.* I slammed out of the chair and paced the cabin.

I'd been outsmarted by this Heveian male. *Me.* An alpha-level agent assassin. I could sneak into the most top-secret places on Earth, but this meathead beat me at my own game.

I couldn't deny it—I was impressed. He was intelligent, resourceful, and pragmatic. I found that combination intoxicating. That didn't mean I liked being stuck in here, *or* the prospect of being stuck in the cruiser's brig. All it did was make me determined to outwit him.

I wasted some time trying to override his locks. That was a fruitless effort. Finally, I gave up, ate some dinner, stewed, fumed, and plotted. He'd left no weapons in the shuttle, of course. Not so much as a butter knife. Time ticked slowly by.

That hour passed. Then, two hours.

Worry curled in my stomach. Something had gone wrong out there. I just knew it. When I'd had this feeling in the past, it had never been unfounded. My instincts were the lucky reason I was still alive after all the missions I had served on.

My thoughts moved to Wulfrex out there, possibly in trouble. Possibly hurt. My belly knotted at the thought. I remembered his hungry kiss and his roughly uttered words.

We'll continue this later.

Be here when I get back.

And how I couldn't promise that I would. I wanted to, though. I wanted *him*. I wanted more than the life I had been living. All at once, my plan changed. My fears of discovery seemed small. I had told him I wanted him to get back to the cruiser alive. I had meant it and I still did.

I was ending up in the brig, anyway. Might as well make sure Wulfrex was alive to put me there.

I wasn't trying to steal the shuttle anymore, but to get out of it and help Wulfrex. I went back to the medical crate I had hidden in and sorted through the contents. I chose a selection of supplies to bring along. Whenever possible, I packed an emergency kit when I knew I would be facing danger. I knew nothing about these alien medical supplies, but I had to assume they were far superior to the bandages and ointments we had on Earth, eh, *back in my day*.

What, exactly, these supplies did, I didn't know, but I packed a selection in a small, collapsible backpack that I had quietly made in the clothing replicator, as well as food and two packs of water. I clipped a compact light to my pack—it was flat and square with a string to attach it to things. The pack strapped around my waist, over my shoulders, and clipped over my chest. I had to treat this like any other mission and be as prepared as possible. The ideal outcome was getting Wulfrex, Axlos, and Ryland back to the cruiser in one piece.

Whatever happened after that, well, I would face the

consequences. They could put me in the brig. I didn't really care anymore. I just knew that I couldn't live with losing Wulfrex. Not like this. Not when there was something I could do to help. To do that, I needed to get out of the ship, which Wulfrex had made very clear, was sealed.

The main entry door was useless. That was obvious, but I tried it anyway. There was always an auxiliary way out. There were always hatches to access other parts of the ship. My challenge would be finding a way out without damaging the ship in the process. We still had to get off this rock and back to the cruiser. Prying open any part that left a gaping hole would destroy our chances of escape.

So, I either had to trick the hatch into opening or find another way out. I didn't have time to fiddle with the hatch. It was alien tech beyond anything I had ever seen before. Instead, I moved to the floor, moving aside crates and containers of supplies to search for other access points. I found one with a yelp of surprise. Toward the rear of the cabin, I located a small panel that offered access to the hydraulics for the landing gear. I wasn't interested in the landing gear, but the opening was large enough for me to slide into.

I didn't have body armor, like the Heveians, which was unfortunate. However, the lack of it made me able to fit into the small space and squirm my way through the narrow gap to find an opening to the outside. It was impossibly tight down here. I had to be very careful not to dislodge any of the machinery that was packed into the space.

Finally, I found an outer access hatch. It was supposed to be opened from the outside, but that was a light obstacle. I still had the fork and I jimmied it into the latch. A few minutes of work, and the panel opened and fell to the floor with a clang. I dropped out lightly onto my feet. The chill in the hangar was bracing. I lifted the panel and reattached it.

When we returned, the interior panel would be easy to replace. The ship would be fine to fly. I shook myself off and stretched again, pleased with my little accomplishment. Wulfrex may have outsmarted me once, but there wasn't a box that had ever been able to hold me.

I didn't have a schematic of the mine, but I did see wet, frost-edged footprints on the stone floor. The Heveians hadn't bothered to avoid stepping in the puddles and the water hadn't evaporated. Rather, it had iced up at the edges, making a clear path across the hangar to where the males had exited. I followed the trail. My soft-soled shoes barely made a sound on the floor as I walked across the cold surface. It was a long way, longer than the length of a football field. I was as ready as I could be to take on whatever was outside the hangar.

I didn't feel ready at all.

Finally, I reached the wall. It was a dark gray, soaring surface that looked impenetrable. The footprints ended at a rough metal door that looked like it had been bashed in a few times and hastily put back in place. It hung loosely and was open a crack. I pushed it open enough to slip through.

Before me was a long tunnel. It was high and wide enough to not feel cramped, but the dark, heavy stone gave an imposing, ominous weight to it. I could hear the dripping of water. The air was damp and cold. Ice crystals sparkled along the edges and corners of the corridor. My breath came in white puffs.

I would've given anything to have a weapon in my hand. Anything would have sufficed. A hunk of metal would've been nice. But all I had was the mangled fork, which I left in my pocket because of the uselessness of it. I held the light aloft and kept moving. The passageway curved this way and that. Here and there, smaller passageways broke off, but I kept on the main one.

I slowed down, listening hard as my senses picked up the first signs of activity. There was movement, shuffling feet. Low vibrations of voices. I hung close to the wall and walked slowly, keeping my footfalls silent.

The tunnel curved to the right up ahead. There was an open space with multiple passageways. Shadows moved. I kept on, cautiously. A figure came into focus. It was an alien of a species unknown to me—which was just about all of them. He wore black armor and carried a blaster. A metal stick swung idly from one of the alien's enormous hands. The being muttered to nobody. I sized up the creature that was about to be my adversary. He was about my height, but bulky, with pasty white scales covering his face. That was the only visible part, not covered by armor. I watched the alien move on two thick, shuffling legs that appeared to end like the blunt feet of an elephant.

The guard was a bad sign. So much for being an abandoned mine, which no one believed was true going into this. But what *was* this? That was a lot of armor and weapons for the guard of a seemingly empty tunnel system.

My heart began to beat fast as my senses went razor sharp. This was my chance of getting a weapon.

The guard walked back and forth through a small space where three other tunnels joined with this one. The metal stick was perhaps the quickest way to get the upper hand. And, of course, I had the element of surprise.

I stayed where I was long enough to be sure that the alien guard's pacing was consistent. Then I moved in slowly and fell into step directly behind. The guard didn't seem to hear me. He continued a slow, shuffling gait. I imagined what this being lacked in speed and agility, he made up for with brute strength and bulk.

I stayed behind the guard for three full lengths of pacing. Then, I nimbly nicked the metal stick from the large hand. It was the length and width of a police billy club.

The guard made a noise of surprise and turned. I moved just as quickly, staying directly behind and out of my adversary's range of vision. The guard raised the hand that had been holding the stick and looked at it, as if puzzled where it went. Then, as he raised his hand to scratch a hairy head, I aimed a jab for the guard's temple, hitting the mark and sending the guard staggering backwards. I struck again, putting my strength and weight behind the heavy metal bar for the massive bridge of his nose, and the guard fell back on his back, out cold.

The whole affair was over quickly, and quietly, which was the key here. Nevertheless, I waited a beat—just a beat—before collecting the weapons. I dragged the guard against the wall and propped him up to make it look like he was sleeping. I wasn't sure if it would work, but it might slow someone down long enough to try to wake him up.

The guard's armor was way too big for me, but I pried off the thick belt and secured it around my waist. It didn't fit, but I cinched it tight and let the long extra piece flap away. I needed a place to store the weapons and the metal bully stick. The blasters I took went right back into their holsters. One was larger and heavier than the other. Both had a full charge. They were advanced and different from the projectile guns I had used last, but the mechanics were the same—aim, pull trigger. Instead of a safety, there was a power switch. I could work with these.

Fully armed, I let out a breath of relief. Now, I was on an even playing field with whoever, or whatever, I encountered out here.

If I was worried about Wulfrex and the others before, I was very worried now. If there was a guard in this empty stretch of hallway, what would be waiting for them when they found their lost Heveian male?

I walked on, determined to find Wulfrex. When I did, I'd tell him the truth. He deserved to hear it and I needed to tell it.

CHAPTER 14

Wulfrex

"This place is like a maze," Ryland muttered.

"It was a mine," I said. "So yes."

"What were they mining for here, anyway?" he asked irritably.

"My guess would be *ashroc* ore and *vistran*, judging by the type of stone here." I flicked a finger over a thin, glinting yellow vein that ran up the tunnel wall. "*Ashroc* mining is often like this, with multiple tunnels that snake around as they chase bands of ore."

"We're headed the right way," Axlos said. "That's all that matters."

As far as I could tell, he was right. The probes had identified the most likely center of activity, where we would hopefully find the Heveian male we had come to rescue. It felt like we had been walking for hours, and there didn't seem to be a direct route to anywhere in this place. Tunnels wound here and there, dead-ending or turning circular.

I could tell that these types of missions were wearing on Axlos. He was older than the rest of us and he'd seen a lot. Leading our little band of rebels could not be easy for him after all this time. And now, with our species' diminished since the disease, I suspected he'd lost his taste for raiding freighters and taking mercenary jobs. I suspected he missed Heveia. I also suspected that he yearned to return there permanently.

As for the rest of us, we would have to decide what we wanted to do. I thought I might not mind some time with my feet on the ground. I had a feeling the others were feeling that way too.

"Coming up to another junction," Ryland said.

There always seemed to be another junction. "Take the right-hand passage," said Axlos.

I thought about what Dani was doing right now. Whether she was behaving herself on the cruiser or cursing me out on the shuttle. Either way, she was safe. At my last check-in, Arria had said she was still in bed. This was a good sign. She needed her rest, because when I returned, I planned to tire her out.

Ryland stopped short and held up a hand. My focus switched to the hard look on his face, and my senses snapped to attention. I could hear it—the slightest sound of movement ahead. We dropped back against the wall. Ryland placed a hand to the side of his helmet and pressed. His face was pure concentration as he listened.

After a moment, he turned to us. "I turned up the volume on my sensor. They know we're here. Seems to be a mix of cybots and hired Laroshian guards."

"Incoming?" Axlos asked.

Ryland nodded. "Prepare yourselves."

We took defensive positions and powered up our blasters. All of us had done this so many times, we didn't need to speak further. We had fought together many times. We had hauled each other out of massacres and patched each other up when things had not gone as planned.

We had been expecting an ambush since something wasn't right here. I hefted my heavy weapon from its massive scabbard on my back, set the charge for full and waited, tense and ready.

Two cybots swung around the corner and my gut tightened. These were not ordinary fighting cybots, but new, battle-designed models being produced in the Facloac quadrant. They were exceptionally lethal. Every part of them was designed to kill. They also had a nasty self-destruct sequence with a dangerous blast range.

The cybots opened fire immediately, spraying blaster fire all around us. It fizzled off our armor, making wafts of smoke curl off our chest pieces with each hit. We fired back, taking one down quickly, but we had to retreat. We backed up into the hallway we had just come from. The cybots were probably programmed to blow if both went down. From what I'd heard, they were designed in teams or pairs. "We take the other bot down, we need to take cover," I shouted above the noise.

The three of us concentrated our fire on the remaining cybot. It fell to its knees, still emitting blasts, but when it fell motionless, we turned and broke into a run. The massive explosion knocked us forward, propelling us straight off our feet. Heat seared my back. If we'd been any closer, we would've been incinerated on the spot. The three of us fell in a heap on the stone floor, skidding on our battered armor.

We struggled to our feet, smelling of hot *plastoid* and plasma fumes.

My ears rang. My body ached. Ahead, Ryland shouted through the dull fog that enveloped my brain.

I looked up to see four more guards ahead. Two cybots and two Laroshian guards.

I aimed my weapon and fired again as my stomach tightened into a knot. We weren't in best form, having just been blown six meters down a tunnel, and we were outnumbered and outgunned. The flaming remains of the two destroyed cybots were still a small inferno.

But we backed up anyway, shooting, dodging what we could, and allowing our armor to absorb hits we couldn't avoid.

Heat was building up in my chest piece. A shot had definitely found a vulnerable spot on my leg, where it burned, and my weapon was overheating.

"Fall back," Ryland shouted.

We did so, each of us taking cover in different tunnel entrances that broke off from the main tunnel.

One of the guards and a cybot concentrated their fire on me. I backed up into the narrow tunnel I'd taken cover in. The walls were very rough and dark. There was no lighting in here and I was alone. Axlos and Ryland had ducked into other passageways. I couldn't see them through the plasma flare, smoke, and clouds of dust.

I hissed in pain as another hit connected with my leg in that same, already injured spot. My knee buckled. I concentrated my fire power on the cybot. It could possibly take out the guard beside it if I damaged it enough, and if Ryland and Axlos were able to disable the one they fought against. It was the only play I had.

I unloaded on the robot, sending a solid stream of plasma at its power center. As I'd hoped, it went down. I was still taking hits from the other guard, however. I could feel pain in other places, but it wasn't enough to disable me. *Not yet.* I turned my now-smoking blaster to the other guard, knowing I only had one or two more shots in it before it had to cool down, when the cybot exploded.

A blast reverberated through the narrow tunnel walls with bone-jarring tremors.

For the second time, I was blasted backwards, only because of the angle I was at, I slammed against the wall and fell to my knees. Heat licked over me. I gritted my teeth against the shock, which quickly abated after the initial blast. But it was a lot to endure. I couldn't hear anything but ringing.

Dirt and rock rained down from the ceiling. A crack stretched out along the floor between my knees. I watched in horror as the crack widened and another one formed. Then, all at once, the floor dropped out beneath me. I fell, along with rock and dirt, to whatever was underneath. I hit the ground. The wind was knocked out of me with the force of being slammed to the floor.

My eyes were filled with grit and I struggled to drag in a breath. All the bones in my body felt shattered. My weapon had flown from my hands. Through the dusty cloud, I saw the red lights of blasters moving towards me.

More guards. Not cybots, but what difference did it make? I was done. I lay there, leg pinned under a rock and defenseless without my weapon. All I could do was watch my impending doom and hope it was quick. There would be no getting out of this one.

I braced myself, teeth bared in a grimace. The Laroshian guards weren't terribly bright, but they were efficient mercenaries, and well-paid ones at that. They wouldn't show mercy, but it would be a quick, clean death at least. That was something.

Suddenly, one of the guards faltered, stumbled and fell to the ground with a grunt of pain. The other one stopped and spun around. There was a movement behind them, a scurrying sound and the red glow of two blasters. The remaining guard turned and peered through the dust-filled corridor.

Thick, yellow slime oozed from the fallen guard. He didn't move. The remaining living guard had his back to me. I'd give anything for my blaster just then. I could end this right now, but whoever was hidden in the shadows was doing just fine. I figured it was Drave. Impatient for word from us, he took it upon himself to come down and join the fight.

Suddenly, a figure dressed all in black leapt from the darkness like a flying *sprix*. Even their face was covered by a black covering, revealing only eyes, which I couldn't make out through the dust and smoke. They held a blaster in each hand and delivered a perfectly aimed blaster shot between the eyes of the Laroshian guard.

It wasn't Drave.

The figure landed on powerful legs and stared down at me. Through the screen of dust, I recognized the figure. A part of me didn't believe it, but I knew that strong, magnificent body. The dark, glittering eyes that gazed down at me.

"Dani?" I croaked.

My hero stepped over the body and closed the distance between us. I knew who it was, even with a mask over her face. There was no mistaking that tall, strong body and the way she moved it.

Dani Ling—the object of all of my desires. Her blasters released twin curls of plasma vapor as she stood before me, like a beautiful, mythological creature.

She stuck her blasters back in their holsters and pulled down her face mask, revealing her stunning, beautiful face. Her gaze ran dispassionately over me. "Hello, Wulfrex," she said. "This is me staying out of trouble."

CHAPTER 15

Dani

Well, that wasn't exactly what I'd expected to happen.

I'd intended to follow Wulfrex and his party at a quiet distance to make sure they were okay. Literally saving his life was not what I'd anticipated in the many scenarios that had run through my head. Now I stood here, looking down on the battered body of Wulfrex, with two dead guards behind me. There wasn't much light in these tunnels. This one was rough and unfinished looking, being even tighter and narrower than the rest, and filthy with debris and dust. The only light came from the adjacent tunnel, which was lit.

I turned on the small, flat lantern on my waist. It

illuminated the rubble-filled passageway. I had to get Wulfrex someplace safe. He was a mess. His armor was warped from taking too many blaster shots. He clearly had a terrible wound on his leg. I hoped the bone wasn't crushed. And somewhere, *hopefully*, Axlos and Ryland were having better luck against the guards. I crouched beside him and felt his pulse as he stared up at me like I was some sort of apparition.

"You…" he breathed.

"Yes, me." His heart worked at a smooth, steady beat. I turned a tight smile on him. "Cute message you left me."

"Didn't work." His voice was slurred. "You're here. How?"

"You didn't check the floor panels."

His eyes went wide but I waved a hand to stop him from getting worked up. "Relax. I didn't damage the ship. I just squeezed out." I moved him around a little, gently, trying to check him over for anything more serious than the leg injury. He had a few blaster burns in the sections of space between armor pieces, but nothing serious. The tips of his long, dark blue hair were singed from the explosions above. I rolled the rock off his leg and examined what was going on there.

"Ow." He winced.

"Yeah, that looks painful." He'd lost an armor piece from his thigh and taken a hit there. His blue blood was a slick mess. I peeled away the torn edges of his pants and tried to see the depth of the wound, but it was impossible without cleaning it out.

His jaw went rock-hard. "It's fine." He shifted his weight as if to get up but I pressed him down.

"It's a fine mangled leg, but still mangled," I said. "You can't walk, right now. I have some supplies. Let me take a look." I pulled the pack off my back and opened it. I pawed through the contents.

Wulfrex craned his neck to see what I was doing. "Did you bring…medical supplies?"

"Yes," I replied. "But I'm not sure how to use them."

"Show me."

I tilted the bag so he could see inside. "That." He pointed to a metal canister with alien symbols on it. "Spray that on the wound. Be generous."

I pulled back more of the torn pants. "Okay, then. Here goes," I said, and then blasted it onto his thigh.

He winced. His hands clenched, but that was it.

"You have good pain tolerance," I said, impressed.

"I knew there was a way to your heart."

I ignored him as the clear solution that blasted with uncomfortable force from the nozzle turned to a green foam. It bubbled up and hissed, then hardened to a flexible, but firm consistency. I poked it and it stayed in place. "Huh," I said. "Interesting."

He grunted. "Now that." He plucked a roll of wide, clear tape from the bag beside me. Jorok had the stuff in his medical lab. It was a thick, skin-like bandage. "Cover the whole thing. No gaps."

I ripped off a piece big enough to cover the green wound and peeled off the backing to reveal a gooey, slimy surface. I placed it over the wound, covering the entire area of the injury. It molded to his skin, clear and secure.

His stunning, light blue eyes fixed on me. His pupils were enormous, round, like a cat's in the dark or when it's scared. "Thank you," he said. "And you're amazing. I should have told you that earlier."

We didn't have time for this. "Look, Wulfrex. They will be sending more guards. Can you stand? Because we've got to move."

Wulfrex nodded to the pack again. "Did you happen to bring some vials with pink stuff in them?"

I found three pink vials as he described in a small black case. I plucked one out and handed it to him. "This?"

"Stars, yes," he said on a sigh. "I'll take that." He grabbed it from me and placed it against his neck, then pushed the dispenser. The pink liquid disappeared into him. He let out a sigh of relief and handed me the empty vile. "That's better."

"Pain medication?"

"Yes. Don't judge. I'm not immortal."

I helped him to a seated position. "I know you're not."

"You want me to walk without sobbing like an infant, don't you?"

I snorted, unable to imagine him doing such a thing over a hurt leg. "Come on. Let's get you up."

He got to his feet with a grimace, but minimal difficulty, and we quickly went through the fallen guards' things for anything useful. I took their communicators and swapped out one of my blasters for one of theirs, which had a better charge. We couldn't carry all of the weapons, so I took the best ones. Wulfrex took two blasters and attached them to his belt. There was a third, which was the biggest and heaviest. I'd planned on leaving it, but he picked it up.

"Where are you going to carry that?" I asked him.

"My back. I lost my good gun." He scowled. "I liked that gun." He locked the weapon into a sheath on his back.

We were in a clearly abandoned mineshaft. It was unused, and hadn't been used for quite some time, except by the guards who did sweeps. I braced my shoulder under his arm and wrapped my arm around his waist to give as much support as I could. His body was huge. I wasn't sure how much assistance I could offer, but maybe just evening out his balance would help.

We hobbled down the tunnel. I kept on the emergency lantern on the lowest setting. It just illuminated what was directly in front of us, but even that was risky. Anyone coming upon us would see the light. But without it, it was too dark to see anything.

"Turn it off," Wulfrex growled. "I have better dark vision than you humans."

I turned off the light and tucked in closer to his side. "I can't see a thing, just so you know," I told him.

"I'll keep you safe," he said.

I resisted the urge to laugh at that. He wasn't keeping anyone safe in his state. The pain killer was helping, but he struggled to put weight on that leg. Whatever medicine was in there might be working, but it took time to heal a wound that bad.

"We need to get someplace to rest your leg and regroup," I said. "Walking on it is only going to make it swell and take longer to heal."

He grunted in response. It didn't need to be said that there was no place to stop right now. We kept going. The tunnel eventually widened. We were going down, deeper into whatever this was. The tunnel was opening, widening more. Suddenly, the smell of the air changed. It was colder, clearer, with a breeze.

"What do you see?" I asked.

"A wide-open space," he said. "Massive. There's mining equipment abandoned and strewn everywhere. Rocks. Bits of ore."

My toe stubbed on a rock. His arm tightened around me, keeping me upright.

"Try to find someplace we can hide for a while," I said.

He began aiming us towards the left. "I see some transports over here. Vehicles. I guess they used them for bringing equipment down."

"Is there anyone else down here?"

"No. It's very abandoned."

I turned my light on to the lowest setting and saw what we were approaching. Ahead, it looked like a line of cylindrical subway cars, with no rails, were lined up. They must've been attached by some advanced magnetics. They were windowless tubes. Some were tipped on their sides. We approached one that was upright.

Wulfrex pried open the door and I shined the light inside. There were long benches in here, as well as some broken containers and junk. It was exactly what we needed.

"It's perfect, let's get in." I helped him over the high lip and we closed the door behind us. I decided I could leave the light on in here and hung it up on a beam that ran along the ceiling. I helped Wulfrex over to one of the benches, which were wide and designed for far bigger beings than either of us.

He pulled off his arm and chest armor, which left him bare from the waist up, then lay down on the length of the bench. I tucked my pack beneath his leg to prop it up. He closed his eyes and let out a long, shaky sigh. "Thank you," he said.

"You said that already." I pulled off the unwieldy belt and dropped it on the floor before sitting next to his head. "But just for fun, what are you thanking me for? Saving your ass?"

"Yes," he said, with a tired, grimy smile. "And for finding a way out of that shuttle." He cracked open an eye and regarded me. "If I had known you were this useful in battle, I would've brought you along."

"If I had known you were this likely to get ambushed, I would've insisted on coming."

He gurgled out a chuckle. "This is the first time *this* has ever happened," he said. "We never get separated. We have endless battle scenarios."

"There was no scenario for this," I said. "Maybe you guys are getting a little too old for this." I wiped my sleeve over his forehead. "I know I am. I was getting ready to retire before my last job."

Those keen eyes fixed on me. "And what *was* your job, Dani? And I want the truth."

There was really no point in hiding it any longer. Especially now, when there was no guarantee that we would get out of here alive. There wasn't. He was badly injured. We were in a completely unknown place, separated from the other Heveians, and by the look of the helmet he wore, the communication link was completely fried. "I was a spy," I said. "You were right about that."

"I knew it." He looked very pleased with himself. "What else? I know there's more."

"And I was an assassin."

CHAPTER 16

Dani

I spoke in a rush, as if that would somehow make it sound less awful. "I worked for a global agency that was formed after the convergence, when the rift opened up that allowed us to travel to the stars and also for different species to visit us. Everything changed on Earth after that. There were governments, corporations, and individuals who wanted to profit from what those other species could offer, even if it meant harm to our own species." I ran my fingers through his hair, which had spilled onto my lap. He wasn't jerking away from my touch. That was something. "The convergence ended a lot of the conflicts on Earth, but it also opened up other problems. Bigger problems."

He watched me with those glittering, slitted blue eyes. "Go on."

I shrugged, unable to come up with a good reason

not to. "Alien tech was entering our world like a deluge, but a lot of it was restricted so it could be studied first and deemed safe. Compared to other species in the galaxy, we are primitive. So the agency I worked for tried their best to stop the abuse of alien tech. Unfortunately, that often meant assassinating those who wouldn't listen to reason and stealing the data or devices they'd illegally gotten." I rubbed a hand over my face and shook my head. "You were right that I know the woman who is still unconscious in Jorok's medical lab. Her name is Dr. Claire Turich. She's a brilliant scientist. She and her partner were researching some of the tech under review, but her partner has a side project."

"A side project?"

"A powerful corporation had given her plans and materials for a weapon that was *not* permitted. It was so dangerous, it could've wiped out entire regions. It was biological in nature, and every law that the global government had put in place forbade these types of weapons in every capacity, *including* research. But Claire Turich's partner accepted the money offered and was working on it in secret." I shook my head. "The woman who was frozen with me knew nothing about it. My job was to take out her partner, which I did. But Claire made an unexpected appearance and saw what I'd done.

"The last thing I remember is locking eyes with her and seeing her accusatory, horrified stare. She looked terrified. And there was this flash of light, and that was it. Then, I woke up to you looking down at me. Fifty-two years later."

Wulfrex let out a low whistle. "That's a bad job, there."

I chuckled. "It was. But it was all I knew."

"Your family didn't encourage you to find a different career?"

"I never knew my parents," I said. "I think they were operatives of some kind, because I grew up in a facility and was trained from a young age to do this work. I went to school, but had this secret life I could tell no one about. There were a few of us like that."

He looked up at me with a soft expression. "So you never knew the love of a family?"

"I never knew love at all." My throat closed around those words. It was a horrible thing to admit. It felt shameful, even though I had not chosen the way I was raised. "It was a time of crisis on our world. I think the agency heads believed that a few kids sacrificed for global security was a small price to pay. Can't argue," I said, as if to justify it.

"I can," he huffed out. "Do you feel better now after telling me that?"

I felt deflated, like an overfilled balloon that finally had its air leaked out. "I'm afraid of what you'll think of me."

He shifted, sitting up beside me while keeping his leg propped up to the side. "I think you're the most amazing female I've ever met in the whole of my life. I think you were doing a service to your people by keeping technology out of hands that could have caused devastation to an unprepared population, even if it might not have been a solution that most would agree with. I think I'm glad you shared this with me, because it hasn't changed my feelings for you one bit."

"But what about the others?" I asked urgently. "When they find out, I'm done. No one wants an assassin on board."

"Do you think we are all so innocent? Do you think *I* have never killed? All of us Heveians have taken lives in the course of our time on that cruiser. Most of them were bad guys, but I can't say for sure all of them were. If you're worried about what the other human females will think, well, I suggest you be honest with them as well. They will surprise you. They certainly surprised us." He narrowed one eye at me. "You still don't think we're brainwashing them, do you?"

I shook my head with a chuckle. "No. I can see perfectly well how any woman could fall in love with you."

His eyes brightened at that. "Are you talking in general terms, or about me?"

"I heard what you said on the shuttle. About what you planned to do with me when you got back."

His expression didn't change at all. "Yes, what do you think of that?"

I glanced over at his leg. "I don't think you're going to be in a position to 'rut,' as you so inelegantly call it, anytime soon."

"Do you know what this stuff is doing to my leg right now?" He pointed at the leg in question. "It's a medicine that is hard to come by, but unbelievably effective. That foam is repairing tissue as we speak. I'll be running laps sooner than you think." He winked. "It won't repair pretty; I'll have a new scar there. Does that bother you?"

I snorted. "You haven't seen my body."

"Jorok has," Wulfrex said. "He mentioned extensive injuries you've sustained, and he showed me a few of them."

"Well, then, you know what I think of scars."

"What do you think of *me?*"

My heart tightened at the bold, blunt question. Since it seemed to be a day of confession, I decided to stay with the theme. "I think about your naked body far more often than I would like," I said. "If things were different, if I had stayed on the cruiser and you returned, I would've welcomed you into my bed."

He leaned back with a sigh, closing his eyes as a serene smile crossed his lips. "It pleases me to hear that."

"But I don't know about the biting thing," I added quickly. "That disturbs me."

"I understand that," he said. "I did a little research on your people. I have learned that the myth of the vampire is quite a figure in stories. I promise you, we are nothing like that. As I said, we do not *drink* blood. A mate that we take blood from means a part of them lives in us forever. It changes us. If you were a Heveian, you would bite me, as well. My blood would run through your veins."

"What about your, ah, genitals?" I wagged a finger towards his crotch. "I assume you have a penis?"

My question seemed to amuse him. He grinned wide and his hands went to the fastenings of his pants. "Do you want to see it?"

I debated, then shrugged, because I was curious. "Yeah. I do."

He wasted no time opening his pants. Out sprung a hard, large cock.

"Oh. Wow," I said before I could take it back. It was different from human male penises. Wulfrex's was long and thick, but shaped like a fleshy corkscrew with a thick purple knob at the end.

He ran a hand idly up the length of it. "What do you think?"

"It's...impressive," I said, taking in the uniqueness of it. "It's different from a human man's. I will say that."

His brows lowered a fraction. "In a bad way?"

"Not *bad*. Just different," I tried to explain. "Humans' are smooth. Yours is not."

"Well, I don't know the particulars, but Drave and Ryland have not expressed rutting problems with their mates, so I am given to understand that humans and Heveians are compatible in that area."

My gaze moved to his face, then back to his engorged cock. "Harp and Kora didn't seem to have complaints."

"Do you want to touch it?" he asked, pointing at his dick again.

I shifted closer on the bench beside him. "Do you want me to touch it?"

"Of course, I do." His eyelids dropped and his gaze darkened. "But it's not going anywhere. Anytime you want, just—"

"I didn't say I didn't want to." I brushed his hand away from his cock and wrapped my fingers around it.

He sucked in a ragged breath and closed his eyes. "Sweet fucking stars," he muttered.

I pulled my hand back, remembering where we were and the condition of his leg. "This is too much for you. I don't want to—"

He grabbed my hand and brought it back to his cock. "You won't hurt me."

"This can't be a good idea." My breath had turned short, shallow. My heart raced.

"Oh, it's a very good idea," he breathed. "My leg is fine. I'm feeling no pain," he murmured. "Touch me."

I swallowed hard as desire moved through me like thick, hot honey. My hand moved over the thick ridges of his corkscrew penis. It swelled in my hand and he arched his hips to increase contact.

"Please," he said. "Can I touch you?"

"Yes." We were sitting side by side, but we had shifted to face each other.

His hand curled around one of my legs and lifted it over the bench so I straddled it. I sat there, legs spread with my hands around his cock and feeling my pussy turn hot and wet. My breath was coming hard.

He cupped my breasts, which weren't huge by any stretch, but swelled at his touch. I arched into him. His big hands slid over my hard, sensitive nipples. He pulled the fabric up and over my head. I was naked from the waist up, suddenly. Cool air licked my skin. I groaned as thick calluses scraped over my skin, igniting me like a spark to gasoline.

He leaned forward and pulled a taut nipple between his lips, nipping gently. His hands slid lower, over my ribs, the gentle nip of my waist, over my hips. Thumbs slid inward and pulled my legs farther apart, then, moved inward more.

I gasped as his fingers found my sex. They pressed there, rubbing against the ache that throbbed and the fire that burned. I struggled to remember that I held his cock. With one hand, I explored his chest. Oh, that wide, muscular chest that gleamed like brushed steel. My fingers slid over the bumps of old scars, puckered and pale.

He slid his hand lower, cupping my sex. His palm rubbed my clit. His fingers pressed into the wet slit that was only inaccessible to him because of my pants. "Take them off," he ordered.

I rose on unsteady legs and unfastened my pants. He held my gaze as I slid them off, shifting my leg over the bench in order to do so. They fell to the floor.

This was madness. I knew it was. It also felt inevitable.

His gaze moved over my naked body, from my face to my feet, then back up again. Lust shone thick and hot in his eyes. "I've wanted you since I cornered you in that maintenance shaft," he said. "I wanted to shove you up against the wall and take you right there in the dark."

I wet my lips with my tongue. "A part of me wanted you to do that, too."

His gaze met mine in a hot, fiery clash. "Ride me," he ordered.

"Like this? Here?"

"We may not have another chance," he said. "I want to know what you feel like. Rut with me, Dani."

He lay back on the bench, one leg on the floor, the injured one stretched out. His cock was a thick rod resting on his stomach. He gripped it and held it upright, waiting for me to impale myself on it.

I couldn't come up with a reason not to. I mean, I *could*. There were a number of perfectly good, rational reasons why having sex with Wulfrex here, in an abandoned transport in the middle of an enemy mine was a terrible idea.

But all of those reasons were also why it felt so exciting. So wickedly intoxicating. And he was right. We might not get the chance again.

The wetness between my legs made it clear which side of the argument my body fell on. My skin was alive with sensitivity, as it always was when he was near, when he touched me. I raised a leg and straddled him, hovering above him and his jutting cock.

His hand slid up my thigh. "Ride me," he said again.

I could smell my own arousal as I positioned myself over him. I slid my wet folds over that thick knob, gasping at the sensations. His cock was now darker purple-blue, engorged, and ready for me. Precum beaded on his tip.

I met his gaze. "This is just sex, right?"

"Oh, Dani," he drawled huskily. "It's much more than just sex."

I paused. A fuck in a crisis combat situation couldn't be anything more. It couldn't. "What is it, then?"

He bared his teeth, showing the frighteningly long, thin fangs. "These tell me that you are my mate, Dani."

My body shivered at the words. *My mate.* He'd said that word before, but I hadn't taken it to mean something big or permanent. He also called sex, *rutting*, which doesn't exactly equate to a life partnership, to my understanding, but he was of an alien species.

I was standing there with the head of his cock lodged in my greedy folds. My body was not going to let me back away now, no matter what he called this thing we were doing. I took a deep breath, pushed all thoughts from my mind, and lowered myself on him, taking in each thick ridge inch by inch. I gasped at the feeling of fullness, the pleasure that rippled up through my body and curled in every nerve ending.

I trembled and he gripped my hips with his massive hands. "Dani," he murmured. "Dani."

To say it was a snug fit would be an understatement.

His dick was bigger than any human man I'd seen, and I'd seen a fair amount in my line of work. I'd ambushed plenty of targets while they were engaged in this activity. Everyone was distracted. Made it easier.

But this was different than any sex I'd seen or participated in. He was large and his cock seemed to be designed to light up my insides like a fucking department store.

He guided me, using his massive hands to lift me up and slowly drop me back on his cock. All my worries dissipated. Pleasure unfolded. His hands moved from my hips to my breasts, squeezing gently, flicking my nipples. I felt alive, so much more vibrant than ever before. This empty transport vehicle was suddenly the most erotic place I'd ever been. I looked down into Wulfrex's slitted eyes. They were open and vulnerable. There was a pinch of concern in them, worry maybe. "Are you okay?" he breathed.

My hands were braced on his wide chest. I placed one on his cheek, then smoothed my fingers over his brow, unknotting the furrow there. "I am fucking amazing," I replied in a ragged whisper. "And so are you."

His hips rose and thrust against me. I gasped and tossed my head back as the pleasure arced through me like an electrical current.

I was going to come. It was a building, pressure-filled need and I knew I wasn't going to be quiet about it.

Just then, he lifted my hand from his chest and brought my palm to his lips. He held my gaze as his mouth moved to my wrist. I knew what he was going to do.

Sharp tips scraped over the skin there. He paused, holding my gaze. "May I?" he asked, deep and guttural.

I bit my bottom lip in a moment of indecision. Did I trust him? Could I trust him with my body? The answer to that was, yes. I wasn't yet sure if I trusted him with my heart, which was completely inexperienced in these matters.

I nodded, excited and a little afraid, as he ran his tongue over the throbbing vein there. "I need to hear you say it," he said.

"Yes," I said. "Bite me. Take me."

He closed his eyes and sealed his lips over my wrist. My pulse beat hard and fast.

There was a prick of pain before it was immediately swallowed up by a shocking wave of pleasure. I gasped and shuddered as ripples and rolls of sensations exploded through me, mingling with the sexual pleasure. It rose to a fever pitch that was almost unbearable.

My back arched. A strangled groan surged from me as my orgasm hit, hard, powerful. My entire foundation shifted. There were two points of intense pleasure—my wrist where his fangs were in me and my pussy where his cock pounded me.

I wasn't even sure it could be called an orgasm at that point. It was more like full-body exorcism, drawing out depths of pleasure I didn't know existed. Throbbing waves of lust pulsed through me, almost punishing in their intensity. I heard a scream, belatedly realizing it was my own. I was pounding him, meeting his thrusts with my own, almost brutal ones.

At last, the torrential storm peaked. I couldn't breathe, couldn't see, couldn't do anything but just fuck him and *feel*. His cock swelled. His balls tightened, and a groan escaped him as he found his release deep inside of me.

Before his mouth released my wrist, he swept his tongue over the tiny marks there, but I didn't care. All I could think about was how to breathe again. How to function again. The waves began to ease. The intensity died back and I slumped over him, boneless and wrung out. Gasping for breath, I buried my face in his neck as the last shuddering waves crashed through me, and then ebbed.

Long fingers slid over my back. I rested my head against a damp chest that moved steadily up and down with the pounding heart inside.

"Shh," said his low, deep voice. "Rest now, Dani."

I was bare-ass naked on top of an injured alien, deep in enemy territory, and I'd never felt so safe and wonderful in my life. I closed my eyes and did as he said, wondering at how easy it was to obey him. Wondering if I would ever be the same again after this.

CHAPTER 17

Wulfrex

Before now, I hadn't given much thought to rutting. Unlike some of my friends on the cruiser, I had indulged in it with females of different species. It was pleasurable. It was a needed release for the body. I had suspected it would be different with Dani. More intense, perhaps. More…something.

I hadn't expected it to be more *everything*.

I cradled the precious female in my arms as she slept. We didn't have long here, but she needed this brief rest. She lay sprawled on top of me in the wake of our rutting. My gums still ached where my fangs had elongated to a length I didn't know was possible.

Her blood was in me. She was a part of me now, and would be forever. I couldn't imagine ever letting her go. At that moment, I couldn't even imagine not being in physical contact with her. I wanted her with me always. And if anything came between us, I would rip it down and tear it to pieces. It was a completely unhinged feeling. Like I had stopped being a civilized Heveian and turned into a barbarian. A beast. A possessive male snarling at anyone who would dare to look at my mate.

I closed my eyes and tried to make sense of the new feelings pounding through me. I wondered if Ryland and Drave felt this way when they first rutted with their mates. Had they turned feral at the new feelings their mates brought out in them?

Dani stirred after a time. She slid over to one side and cuddled against me, drawing her knees up and tucking her face against my neck. The bench was wide enough when I moved over a little. My shoulder was her pillow. Her soft breasts rested against my ribs. Her long, strong thighs leaned against mine. One arm stretched across my chest languidly. Her fingers played with the burned tips of my hair.

We smelled like plasma fumes, burnt *plastoid*, and sex. Those first two things should not have been appealing—*they weren't*—but we could have been surrounded by garbage and it wouldn't have dampened the arousal flooding me.

"We need to get up," she said in a gravelly voice. "I need to check that leg."

"It's fine," I said. I couldn't remember how many times I had said that about an injury. Too many times to count. Sometimes it really was fine. Sometimes it wasn't. But it was always fine until we were back on the cruiser and Jorok could take a look at it and patch me up.

In this case, my leg really was fine. Dani had dressed and covered it quickly and I could feel the skin knitting, stitching itself back together. It itched. That was a good sign of healing.

"*You're* fine." She nipped my shoulder, then sat up. The chin-length swing of her hair fell around her face. "You really are."

I folded my hands behind my head and grinned up at her. "Glad you're finally coming to your senses."

"Hmm. And cocky." Her gaze moved appreciatively over me, pausing at my semihard cock, then continuing down to the wound on my leg. Her fingers gently moved around the edges of it where the synthetic skin had covered the rapid-healing foam dressing. "The redness has gone down," she said. "The foam has changed color." She looked at me curiously. "Is it supposed to do that?"

I nodded. "It will lose its color and turn white as the healing properties do their work. When it's completely white, it can be removed."

"How bad does it hurt?"

I lifted my leg, experimentally bent my knee and flexed. There was a dull ache to it, but it was very mild in the scheme of things. I nodded. "Much improved, thanks to you."

She shrugged. "It's what you do."

"Yes, but I mean, remembering to bring medical supplies. None of us did." I stretched my arms and yawned. "Come to think of it, we never bring medical supplies into battle. We leave it on transports or drag ourselves back to the cruiser."

Dani's hand slid up my chest. "Well, you Heveians are all sturdier than the average human, I think. And you have this armor." She nodded at the chest piece that lay on the floor beside us. "I've never seen anything withstand hits like this stuff."

"It's *plastoid* reinforced with a few special additions. It's saved our lives more than once." I gazed at the warped pieces I would have to wear again. "I wish I could give it to you. I would, if it would fit."

"No way." She laughed. "If I were to try, it would be like wearing a giant turtle shell. These pieces were clearly made for you. You're the only one who could wear it. It would even be too big on your crewmates."

I grunted and sat up, dragging the transparent chest piece over to me and running a hand over the uneven surface. It was blackened in areas. The heat of repeated blaster shots had managed to warp the strong material. It was beyond repair and would be discarded after this mission, but in the meantime, I pulled it on and clasped it at the sides, front and back.

Our delightful interlude was over. It was time to get back to the business of survival, finding Ryland and Axlos, and getting out of this miserable mine with our rescued Heveian.

I watched Dani dress with faintly concealed regret. I wanted to rut with her again. There were two slight marks on her wrist from my teeth. They were tiny, just a smudge of discoloration. I had marked her. Little did she know, I had claimed her as mine. "Did I hurt you there?" I asked hesitantly, pointing to her wrist.

She looked surprised, then glanced down at the marks. "No. I'd forgotten about it." She slid her fingers over the light red marks. "Your saliva had more than pleasure enhancers in it if these closed up so fast."

"Our fangs get very thin," I said. "And yes, our saliva contains an antiseptic. We don't want our mates getting infections from our bites."

"Makes sense," she murmured, bending to pull on her boots.

If we got out of this alive, things would be different between us, and since she had told me the truth about her past at last, we could dispense with all the secrets and subterfuge.

We took a moment to eat a few rations from her bag and have a drink of water before creeping to the door of the transport. Dani cracked it open the slightest bit and peered out. "It looks as empty as before," she said.

I slid my helmet over my head and engaged the visor. It had a setting that allowed me to scan for heat signatures. It was barely working, having been damaged by the battle like the rest of the components. Still, as I looked out into the giant cavern where extensive mining had occurred, the scanner caught a slight signal.

"I'm seeing a slight tail, probably from a scanning drone," I said.

"Did it come over here?"

"Doesn't look like it. It appears to have done a quick loop and left, but this thing is only showing a partial view. The rest of it was damaged from the heat."

She fastened her blasters on her belt. "We see one, we shoot it down."

"You don't have to tell me twice. I hate those things."

"Can you connect with the cruiser? Maybe now that your helmet has cooled off, it can reestablish a connection."

"No," I said with a wince. "The circuitry is completely burned out. I should have increased the insulation. Or installed a backup system in case of something like this," I muttered to myself, annoyed.

"You can't prepare for every single possible calamity," she said.

"It's my job to."

"Well, then, your job is impossible," she replied pragmatically, tightening the belt around her waist. There was a long extra flap of it dangling in front of her.

I pulled a knife out of my leg piece. "Hold still." I sliced it off and tossed it aside. "That's better."

She looked down and smiled. "Thanks. That's been bothering me."

"Glad to take one off the list."

The smile faded. "Look, Wulfrex, I don't know what to think of what we just did. Maybe it was in response to the danger we were in. Maybe—I don't know. But I can't think about it right now. It *was* just sex."

Without thinking, I took her chin in my hand and

turned her face to mine. My expression was fierce, I knew it. My blood still pumped hard and hot. "It was not just sex," I growled. "It meant something. To me. To you. And I will not allow you to denigrate what we just shared to 'just sex.' You are mine."

Her eyes flared. Rebellious light sparked in their depths, but also a flash of arousal. She did not jerk her face out of my grasp. She stared at me with those complicated eyes, full of conflict. "We'll see, Wulfrex. Let's get out of here first."

I could not argue with that. Completing this mission was paramount to any discussions of feelings, even though my emotions demanded they be moved up in the priority list.

I dropped my hand, and nodded. "But we *will* discuss this when we are back on the cruiser."

I moved past her to the cracked-open door of the derelict transport. There were no active surveillance drones out there presently. I was in rough shape on the way here and so I wasn't sure how we got here. And I had no idea how to get out.

We slipped out of the transport, turning off the lantern and plunging ourselves into darkness. I gathered her close to my side, knowing she was blind in this environment. "All I know is, we need to go up," I said.

I preferred not to go back the same way we came, considering the instability of the tunnel, and the likelihood of it being swarmed by guards or drones. Instead, I worked my way around, guiding Dani carefully, until

I found a tall, metal ladder leading up, to where, I didn't know.

"How high does it go?" she asked, feeling the rungs with her hands.

"I can't see the top." I peered up, straining my eyes, trying to see, but it was in darkness. Even my eyes could not locate the top.

She shrugged. "Well, let's go. Options are limited."

I liked how pragmatic she was. No fuss. No crying.

We started climbing with her in front of me. Each rung of the ladder clinked beneath our feet. I couldn't see around her, so I still did not know when we would reach the top. But finally, Dani paused and turned to look down at me. "I think we're here."

I climbed over her, my chest to her back, and looked over her shoulder at the tunnel before us. It was dark and empty, snaking off to some unknown destinations.

"It's empty," I said. "Climb up."

Neither of us looked back over the deep, gaping pit behind us as our feet settled on solid ground again. This tunnel was rounded and large, as if it had once been frequently used. There had been lifts built in, which had once brought supplies up and down here. They were broken and moldering, now, a testament to how long ago this area of the mine was occupied.

We started up the passageway, hands on weapons, walking as quietly as we could. Something about this area made me certain that it was no longer completely abandoned. The farther we walked, the more I felt sure of this. We were getting close to something. Something important.

Suddenly, Dani grabbed my arm and yanked me against the wall. We flattened there. She flicked me a glance and squeezed my hand. "Movement up ahead."

I heard it now. The slightest scuffle, but it was getting louder. There was movement in the shadows.

We each drew a weapon and moved quietly and stealthily down towards the commotion. We almost tripped over the body of a guard. We stepped around it and kept going. Sounds were getting louder. We picked up our pace. There were lights on the ceiling, running along the top in a pale green glow.

Tension radiated from Dani. It matched my own. Around the corner, the noises were louder—voices, blaster shots, the skid of rocks. There was a battle going on. I looked at Dani and nodded. She nodded back grimly and we both made our move together.

We looked around the corner to see two beleaguered Heveians battling hard against at least six guards.

Axlos and Ryland were giving it everything they had. Axlos limped. Both of them were struggling to hold their positions. Their weapons smoked. Their armor was more warped and discolored than mine.

Together, wordlessly, Dani and I stepped out from our location and joined the fight.

Ryland and Axlos started in surprise. I had no time to spare them more than a quick look, but I could sense the relief washing over them. Dani and I had full charges on our weapons. We were alert and rested, which was more than I could say for my Heveian brethren, who looked ready to fall over.

I positioned my body in front of Dani's as much as possible. She had no armor at all. A direct hit could kill her. She did not miss a beat, aiming around me with precision that made my heart swell with pride. This was *my* female, who was a better shot than any Heveian on the cruiser—even Ryland, who was magnificent. Despite not having much time to study her enemy, Dani made quick work of discovering where their weak points were. She aimed for disabling first—knocking blasters out of hands and finding gaps in armor. The two cybots were brought down last. They exploded in dramatic fashion. With the enemy neutralized, we ran, joined by Axlos and Ryland.

Axlos stared, perplexed at Dani, but said nothing about it. "Nice timing," he said, panting.

"As usual," I said, then nodded ahead to where the burning remains of our attackers lay. "Where is our destination?"

Ryland nodded. "Up there. I'm the only one with a working com. Jorok and Drave sent down probes to try to find you in the mine. Drave is worried sick. He's preparing a crew to come down."

"Tell him not to," I said, realizing that the drones I detected in the open cavern were probably from the cruiser. "Let's get this done and get out of here."

Ryland's gaze hung on Dani. "I want an explanation for this later," he said. "But that was some incredible work you just did."

"Thanks," Dani said. "I've had some practice."

"This story will be fascinating." He motioned ahead, then looked at her inquisitively. "You are good to continue?"

She nodded. "Like Wulf said, let's get this done."

"Stay behind us," said Ryland to her, then to us, "Keep her behind us. She has no armor."

We moved ahead with more speed now. The lights were new, I realized. There was no flickering or broken bits that would indicate that the lighting was part of the original mine system. They became lighter, brighter. The hallway turned larger, smoother, and cleaner as we moved down it.

"We think the facility is this way," Axlos said.

"What happened to your leg?" I asked.

He grunted in response. "I could ask the same of you. Where'd you find medical supplies?"

"Dani thought to bring them." I shook my head. "Which begs the question why *we* never bring them."

"We don't usually need them," said Ryland.

"We did this time," I muttered. "If it weren't for her, I would be dead right now."

Ryland placed a hand to the side of his helmet and filled Drave in on what was happening down here. A flicker of a smile moved over his face. "Drave says he'll stay on the cruiser for now. But he's ready."

We reached the end of the corridor, which ended in a big metal door. Definitely not part of the original mine. It was locked, unsurprisingly, but I found the control pad under a metal plate beside it and rigged the controls to make the door open. We held ourselves tense and ready on either side of the doorway as the metal door swung open. We stepped inside, ready for anything.

I couldn't speak for anyone else, but my jaw dropped. It wasn't just a laboratory in here, it was a large installation. Shelves of plants, illuminated by a rich, purple light, lined one wall. Massive slab tables, filled with devices and instruments, crowded the center of the room. And the room was cavernous, almost as expansive as the large mining pit we had just left. Perhaps that's what this had been, once.

We crept inside cautiously. There were no signs of anyone, which made me more nervous than if we had walked into an ambush. Everything was pristine. Clean. It smelled pleasant and tinged with the bright scent of the plants growing on their lit shelves. We walked in farther.

Vats of clear liquid lay placed in rows. They were large enough to hold a being of our size. Mechanical parts took up the next section of the chamber. Metal fabric-replication units sat stacked and giving off heat. Pieces of machinery that I identified as the elements that made up a cybot, hung from racks. "They're manufacturing their own cybots here," I said. "Look at this." I gestured to a molded shape that was the rudimentary form of a cybot arm.

Ryland shook his head. "I don't think that's what they're doing," he said grimly. He gestured to another area that contained a vast amount of medical equipment. Disturbing instruments that only came out occasionally in Jorok's medical lab sat out on trays.

A chill ran through me. We kept going. I dreaded what we might find. Finally, we reached a massive dark cell. Thick bars formed a wall along the rear. Behind it, things shifted in the darkness. A foul stench filled our nostrils as the four of us gazed into what lay beyond those bars.

"What's back there?" Dani whispered to me.

"Prisoners," I said tightly. "I count fourteen."

"Do any of you see our Heveian?" Axlos asked.

"Not yet. Only one way to find out if he's hiding in the back," Ryland said, holstering his weapon. He removed from his belt a knife that gave off an electrical charge. It was quite useful in close-combat situations, delivering a healthy shock. In this case, he turned it on to full power and jammed it into the locking mechanism. Sparks exploded from the lock, hissing against the bars in the floor.

Ryland put the knife away and pulled open the door. "Be ready for anything," he said.

Dani took out her lantern and turned it on. It illuminated the cell and we could make out the life forms in here clearly. A range of species was represented. All of them were in poor condition. Ragged lumps, either huddled in corners or standing menacingly still as we moved into the cell. Dani swung her light in a slow arc. It lit upon dull gray skin against the back wall.

"You there," Axlos called. "You're Heveian."

The male did not move. He stayed where he was. He

appeared to be guarding something as he hunched against the wall in a defensive stance.

"We're not here to hurt you, mate," I said. "We came to bust you out."

Still, the male did not move. We made our way forward. Maybe he couldn't hear. The closer we got, the more we saw of this male. Ryland let out a harsh curse under his breath. Metal gleamed on the Heveian prisoner where an arm and a leg should have been.

"Fucking stars," Ryland murmured. "What have they done to him?"

CHAPTER 18

Dani

I could empathize with the Heveians' shock at seeing one of their own like this. The male was a mess. I wasn't an expert on cybernetic parts, but even I could see the job that had been done on this poor guy was awful. He had a metal arm from the shoulder down and definitely one of his legs was metal. His head was shaved and marked by surgical scars. Some were fresher than others. There was a metal patch over one eye and who knew what else lay under the ragged clothes he wore. His one good eye glared at us with a hostile gleam.

I wasn't sure if my companions could recognize it, but this guy wasn't in his right mind. Whoever this Heveian once was, it wasn't who he was *now*. I wasn't sure if these three were picking up on that. And I didn't think they were paying attention to the thing that this male was trying to protect. I barely caught it myself, or rather, *her*.

Huddling behind this hulking cyborg was a human woman. She was tiny in comparison to him, also dressed in rags, and was utterly filthy. She had a small gray oval face and dark, limp hair that hung around her face. She peeked around the side of him with big, dark eyes. Our gazes met for a split second, before hers moved to my raised weapon, and she ducked out of sight behind the male cyborg.

Meanwhile, these three were trying to reason with him.

"Come on, we're going to leave," said Wulfrex, with a hint of frustration. "You don't want to *stay* here, do you?"

Ryland looked nervously back towards the open cell door. Other prisoners were edging towards it. Whether to leave, or block our exit, I didn't know. I caught Ryland's eyes. "Someone's got to watch that exit," I murmured.

He nodded and chose himself to go back there. I saw him speak to a prisoner that approached. It didn't look like it was turning hostile, but rather, Ryland was asking the prisoner something.

I turned my attention back to the problem before me. I didn't like this. This male was preparing to attack. Any second, he was going to lunge.

"Hey," I said to Wulfrex. "Give him a little space."

He looked at me, perplexed. "I'm not sure he can understand us."

"I don't think he can. All the more reason to give him space." I nudged him. "Look at this guy. He's about to blow."

Wulfrex winced, but Axlos held up his hands and gestured towards the open door where Ryland was in conversation with a different prisoner. He switched his language from the common galactic tongue to Heveian, which caused my translator to pause and recalibrate before I could understand what he was saying.

I missed part of it, but I heard "home," and that seemed to sink in with the cyborg, at least, a little.

A small, pale hand reached out and curled around the male's bicep. She emerged cautiously, peeking around and gaping at Axlos and Wulfrex.

"Stars," Axlos murmured. "Another human."

The cyborg looked down at her. His nostrils flared and his expression turned desperate, wild.

Shit, I thought. He thinks we're here to take the female. He has no idea what we're saying.

"Hey," I said to the woman. "Tell him we're not—"

But before I could finish, the cyborg lunged towards them. It was almost sad to see. The male's right leg had no joints. It was one piece of hulking metal that looked as if it had been put together with random scraps. It didn't look remotely like a leg, but rather, like a sick experiment gone wrong.

He hobbled forward on his awkward leg, relying on his organic leg for most of his mobility. Still, he might have had a monstrosity of a peg leg, but he was powerful and strong. A rough, skeletal metal fist curled and swung out, barely missing Axlos' face.

"Back off, now," said Wulfrex, sending a warning shot to the floor in front of him. It did not stop the Heveian cyborg's advance. He lurched forward on his normal leg, dragging his ungainly, mismatched one behind him. It was too long for his body. He bared his teeth and snarled.

"Oh, this is wonderful," Wulfrex quipped. He looked at Axlos with confusion. The unspoken words between them were, *we can't fire at him.*

But even then, the furious cyborg continued towards them.

This is some rescue attempt, I thought wryly, as my mind searched for another plan. The cyborg had left the female unattended. He didn't see me as a threat, despite my weapon. He had trained his attention on the two Heveians.

I slunk back and grabbed the woman. She yelped and stared up at me in terror. She was nothing but skin and bones dressed in a long, stinking rag. "We're trying to get you two out of here," I said. "But your boyfriend's making that hard."

"He's not my—" She cut herself off with a whimper. "He's just trying to protect me."

"I get that. Tell him to back off," I ordered.

"I—I can't. He doesn't understand words."

"Fuck," I muttered, then turned the woman around and clamped her back to my side. "Just play along," I gritted in her ear. "And sorry about this."

She was shorter than me, which wasn't uncommon. I was taller than most women. I looked over her head at what was going on.

The cyborg's focus was still on Axlos and Wulfrex. I dragged her into the cyborg's line of vision. His eye widened on me and he lunged forward. The woman began to squirm, probably because I was gripping her too tightly. I loosened my hold a little, but I could see that this was escalating.

I pulled my small blaster and held it to her head. "Keep it together," I snarled at her. "We're trying to get out of here alive."

She whimpered, trembling in my grip. "C-can you put the gun away?" she stammered out.

"I'm not going to hurt you, but your boyfriend needs to think I will," I said. "I don't know what else will get him to stand down.

"Hey," I shouted. Everyone stopped and looked at me. The cyborg stared at me with an agonized expression. He shook his head and reached a hand weakly towards the woman.

"What's your name?" I asked her.

"Kiki," she said.

"Kiki, tell this guy we're here to help him and get him out of this stinking place. Communicate any way that works. We're not the enemy."

I lowered the weapon and released her, hands out. Kiki stepped away from me and ran over to the cyborg. He raised his organic hand and placed it on her shoulder. She leaned close to him and patted his arm. She rubbed soothing circles on his forearm. The cyborg's expression shifted. He looked uncertain, but did not resume his fighting stance. She took his hand in hers and gestured towards the open cell door.

Wulfrex looked at me, eyebrows raised.

The Heveian cyborg's eye moved over the three of us with suspicion and an edge of panic.

We moved as a group towards the open cell door. Ryland wasn't stopping anyone from leaving, which meant the prisoners were streaming out. They were weak and haggard. Some had metal parts, like the Heveian. There were different species and all of them seemed happy to leave.

We reached Ryland. He stood at the ready, weapons drawn, but none of the other prisoners were bothering him.

"What's going on here?" Axlos asked him.

Ryland shrugged. "Common story. Abduction. Imprisonment. Experimentation. These are the few that have survived what went on here." He jerked his head toward a small control panel. "They can send for help here. We need to leave."

As we left, I stayed close to the woman. "You're going to have to talk some sense to this guy," I said to her. "We're getting on a shuttle and returning to a larger ship. You both can get medical attention there."

"He can't speak," she said. "They did something to his brain, as well as his body."

I winced and watched as the cyborg hobbled on his straight metal leg and kept his eye warily on the

Heveians. This woman, Kiki, was the only one who could calm him, it seemed.

"Did you know him before they did this to him?" I asked.

"He was here when I arrived, but he wasn't quite as gone as he is now. They…worked on him more than the others." She shook her head, looking agonized. "We protect each other."

"I'm relying on you to keep him from attacking my friends again," I said.

The woman nodded and ran a soothing hand over her cyborg protector's arm. She looked at me hopefully. "You can really take him home?"

I shrugged. "Easier than getting us home."

Our gazes met in a raw moment of shared trauma. I couldn't imagine what she had gone through in that cell. If her smell was any indication, it had been hell.

I moved to Wulfrex's side as we passed through the mechanical area of the lab installation. The cyborg's eye rolled towards the vats of liquid and large tables, covered in straps and chains, and the parts littering the floor and lining the walls on hooks. He made a guttural, moaning noise, and his steps faltered. "Good god," I breathed. "This guy is so traumatized he can barely function," I said.

"Not only trauma. See the scars on his head? Neural blocks. Intended to wipe him clean and mold him into…something else." Wulfrex had a scowl plastered to his brow. "It wasn't what we expected."

It couldn't have been. This really wasn't a Heveian

anymore. This poor soul had been warped and twisted into something else. "Your physician is going to have his work cut out for him," I muttered.

Wulfrex looked down at me. "So will I. He can't go around like that. I'll have to work on his—"

He was cut off by the sudden appearance of a small group of beings who had emerged from a modest room that we had overlooked.

"What are they?" I snapped, immediately aiming my weapon at them.

"*Kloogs*," Ryland hissed out. "Should've fucking known."

They were guiding a drugged alien prisoner with bandages covering a blue head, and had not expected their prison to be opened and the inmates set free. Some of the prisoners advanced. Axlos grabbed one of the Kloogs and propelled him to the side of the room. "What is going on here?" Axlos asked.

The little being, with a slit-like mouth and huge, yellow eyes, blinked up at Axlos, trembling in terror. "Our orders," he stammered out.

"What orders?" Axlos gave the small creature a shake by the front of his white garment, which was clenched in his fist. "*What* were you doing here?"

"Testing equipment," he said. "They want cybot hybrids."

"Who wants this?" Axlos demanded through gritted teeth. "Who hired you?"

The little creature shook his head frantically.

Wulfrex joined Axlos, gazing down impassively at

the little being. "You might as well tell us," he said. "The instant we let you go, the other people you tortured will be on you. We can call them over now, if you like."

Around us, the other prisoners were attacking the Kloogs. A few of them scurried away, locking themselves back in their room. But it didn't end well for a few others.

"It was the UCP," the Kloog said. "Chancellor Wisklar hired us to do this."

"What were you planning to do with the human?"

"Nothing." The small creature bared pointed, yellow teeth. "We were supposed to get two more of them to work on the same way as the others, but they didn't arrive. That one was different." He rolled his big eyes toward Kiki. "Wisklar wanted its blood analyzed, but canceled the job. We were stuck with it, but it kept the Heveian in line."

It. I felt sick to my stomach, hearing this alien talk about ordering up humans like a fast food order. "You're torturing the people in here," I snarled.

The small, pale, green-skinned alien blinked his massive yellow eyes up at me. "They're subjects, not people. All of the species here belong to worlds that the UCP has or will conquer. They want hybrid, organic cybot fighters to keep the people in line or to exterminate them."

My lip curled, and I raised my weapon right at the alien's face. "The UCP will never take over Earth," I said.

The little creature's thin mouth stretched into a grotesque smile. "It already has."

"Liar." My finger tightened on the trigger. Anger and fear burned in my chest. Then, a large hand rested atop my weapon and lowered it.

I turned to look up at Wulfrex gazing calmly down at me. "Easy, little human."

"We're taking this one alive," Axlos said.

Wulfrex shrugged. "Looks like we'll have an occupant in the brig, after all."

Axlos moved the creature to his side. The cyborg gazed down into the Kloog's face, who sneered up at him.

"We were just getting somewhere with you," the Kloog snarled, then dipped a hand in his pocket. In the quickest of moves, he withdrew a tiny vial containing a black liquid. He moved fast, aiming to jab it into the cyborg, but didn't make it.

The cyborg raised his metal fist and slammed it into the small alien's head. He dropped like a stone. The vial rolled out of his hand. I picked it up and tucked it in a pocket.

"Ah, well," sighed Wulfrex. "Looks like the brig stays empty. Still, we'll get the data," Wulfrex said. He reached into one of his own pockets and pulled out a small metal disc, which he stuck to the side of the control panel. "Will take a while, but this will scan everything on here and transmit it back to the cruiser."

We moved through passageways that Ryland and Axlos had already been down. The cyborg took more time to move than we did. It slowed our progress, but most of the guards had been cleared out earlier.

I exchanged a glance with the woman, Kiki. I was probably as alien to her as any of the other life forms in this place. She was glued to her male's side. His organic arm around her shoulders. She looked up at me. I was beginning to see the spark that was a likely indicator of her underlying strength. "What is your name?" she asked me.

"Dani," I said. And jerked my chin towards the lumbering male beside her. "What about him? Do you know his name?"

"He couldn't speak when I arrived," she said. "So I don't know."

We turned a corner. I was beginning to recognize these tunnels. We weren't too far from the hangar. The other prisoners had dispersed. I hoped they'd find transports in another part of the mine, or send a communication back home. I guessed Wulfrex would send out a signal about the mine. There was certainly more to this facility than it appeared, but we didn't have time to explore it. Not with all the injuries in our party and two rescued people to evacuate.

"Why is he protecting you?" I asked Kiki.

"They threw me in this cell and I was immediately sat upon by other prisoners. He beat them off and protected me ever since. I took care of his injuries, whenever they…did something to him. I kept his wounds clean," she said. "After they…did things to his brain, he remembered. I was his lifeline, I guess." She swallowed hard. "And he was mine."

Bile rose in my throat at the thought of what these two had endured. "And I thought my life was hard," I muttered.

I didn't know how this woman was still upright. There was nothing to her. She was malnourished. She looked beyond exhausted. Yet here she was, walking alongside the terrifying alien who had saved her life god knows how long ago.

"Sorry about the gun-to-the-head thing," I said. "It wasn't personal."

She didn't even have the energy to smirk, but I could tell she wanted to. "Thanks for saving us. I don't think he would've lasted much longer."

My gaze went sharp on her. "I don't know how you lasted this long."

"I grew up fast," she said. "In a hard place. You learn to survive."

Yes, you do.

There it was ahead. The rough, battered metal door that opened to the hangar. Just a little bit farther. I almost let out a sigh of relief.

Almost.

Ryland opened the door and was immediately smacked in the face by an armored fist.

More fucking guards had been waiting for us in the hangar.

They had the element of surprise, this time. Blaster shots rained down on us. Wulfrex thrust me behind him as he fired at the attackers. They were well armored this time. The cyborg put himself in front of Kiki, and once again adopted his fighting stance. He had no weapons, aside from himself, until Wulfrex thrust a spare blaster in his hands. The cyborg looked like he didn't know what to do with it for a moment, then began shooting like the rest of us.

I took my usual position behind Wulfrex and returned fire. There were only four of them. We could do this.

Suddenly, heat seared my upper arm. I hissed and turned around. There were *four more* guards closing in from behind. The shot hit me in my dominant arm, but I could still use the other one. I swung around and returned fire. The cyborg had good aim. He took down one of the guards and turned on another one.

Wulfrex spread his arms and shot in both directions. My weapon was running out of charge. I tossed it aside, and reached for the other one in my holster. It was heavier and I was tired, but I raised it and unloaded on our attackers.

I didn't like the odds all of a sudden. Even with the cyborg helping, they were closing in on both sides. Another shot sent sizzling pain on my shin. *I had no armor.* Axlos and Ryland appeared to be making progress with the group in the hangar. They protected me as well as they could with their bodies, but shots still made it through.

Wulfrex turned to me, but at that moment, I took a direct hit right to the abdomen.

I went down, doubled over, dropping my gun as pain seared through me. The guard, with his pasty white skin and jutting tusks, loomed over me. All I could see was the blaster muzzle right in my face. Plasma fumes curled from the muzzle. I squeezed my eyes shut, but just as I did so, a massive body hurled itself over me, and an armored foot slammed into the guard.

Wulfrex stood there, shouting at me, but everything I heard was a cacophony of noise. My vision turned fuzzy and gray. I curled on the floor, closing my body around the excruciating pain. Voices shouted. Blasters sent flashes of light through my closed eyes. I tasted metal in my mouth and my extremities went numb.

Massive arms came around me and lifted me up. I could feel Wulfrex's heart pounding through his *plastoid* armor. "You'll be okay," he murmured.

"This is bad," I whispered, because it was all I could do. "Really bad." I'd been injured enough times to know.

"No," he said. "You're staying with me." His voice broke. We were moving, rapidly. Voices around me were urgent and sharp.

"I'm sorry," I breathed. "So sorry."

"You've nothing to be sorry for," he said brusquely.

"I do. I should've told you the truth." My voice was slurred. I felt so cold. I was hanging onto consciousness through sheer will. My body itself felt like it was shrinking. Dematerializing.

"You did tell me the truth. And I still love you."

Tears pricked my eyes. "No one's ever said that to me before."

"I'm saying it now. And I want to say it to you again every day for the rest of our lives, so you better fucking stay alive."

I smiled. "Just in case, I love you, Wulfrex."

And that was it. I slipped under in his arms as he raced back to the ship. The world went black and warm and quiet.

CHAPTER 19

Wulfrex

"We are fucking saving her," I snarled, voice ragged. *Everything* ragged.

Axlos looked pained, and not because he was a mess of injuries. His gaze fell to the large gaping wound on Dani's belly. He said nothing, but slid into the operator seat himself and set the controls to deliver us back to the cruiser.

I crumpled to the floor, holding her in my arms, knowing nothing in the medical crates could help her. Not really. But I barked out instructions to Ryland for the things that might slow the bleeding until we got back to the cruiser. He dug into it, pulling out materials.

"Let me see it," he said.

I shuddered and unfolded her enough to reveal the horrible wound.

Ryland drew in a sharp breath. Her skin was obliterated. Her internal organs were visible through the welling blood.

"Use the whole sheet of black wound covering over it," I ordered. "That'll stop infection, and keep her from bleeding out until we get her to Jorok." My cheeks were wet. I pulled her close again and rocked her. Her skin was the color of ash. Her body was limp. I could feel her pulse, weak and thready.

"Anything else?"

I thought about what Jorok had put in that crate for us. "See if there's an orange syringe with a blue cap. It slows down the body's functions. Useful with severe injuries. Should slow the bleeding…inside." My voice broke.

Ryland found what I asked for and injected it into her neck. "We'll be back soon." He squeezed my shoulder. "She's strong. She'll make it."

The Heveian male we had rescued, gazed at us with a surprisingly tender expression. His gaze moved over me, then to Dani, then back to me. He nodded slowly.

He was, thankfully, calm. No longer trying to fight us, which would've been a disaster on the ship right now. I wasn't capable of anything. Axlos was on his last bit of energy, leaving Ryland as the only one able-bodied enough to do anything. He set up an intravenous drip to deliver fluids to Dani as I held her there, murmuring words of love, words of hope.

"Jorok will be able to do something," Ryland said fervently. "He saved our whole species from a disease by making untold numbers of cures. He can help her."

I nodded. I couldn't speak. I couldn't even find the will to put words together. All that mattered was this female in my arms. This beautiful, powerful creature, who had never known love. And there was me, who had known it my whole life. My family had loved me, my crewmates were my best friends, and I knew we loved each other. But Dani…

I wanted to give her a life of love. I wanted to show her a new way to live. And despite all the love I had in my life, I had lacked a purpose. I had joined up with my friends on a lark, and it remained a lark until I met her.

Now, all I wanted was to protect her, please her. But I couldn't do any of that if she was dead.

Ryland handed a pack of water to the female who sat beside the cyborg. He handed her a damp cleansing cloth to clean her hands. Instead, she reached over and dabbed it over Dani's dirt-streaked face. She cleaned the grime from my mate's skin so tenderly, I looked up at her curiously. "Why? You are dirtier than she is."

"She needs it more than I do," said the female.

She had told Dani her name, but I had missed it. I didn't have the energy to ask any more questions. My own injuries were beginning to catch up to me. Throbbing aches, pains and shortness of breath, thanks to all the fumes I'd inhaled. I coughed, being careful not to jostle Dani.

In the front seat, I saw Axlos with his head rested back against the chair in exhaustion. I exchanged a look with Ryland. A communication passed between us. We couldn't do much more of this. Maybe we *were* just getting too old. Maybe we were just no longer cut out for these kinds of missions, filled with shoot-outs and explosions. All those close calls were catching up with us.

I closed my eyes as tears rolled down my face. The life of my beautiful mate faded as I held her in my arms. The rest of the journey back to the cruiser passed in a blur of worry and hope.

We docked in the hangar and I wasted no time in hurrying out with my precious bundle. I gritted my teeth as I squeezed us both into the air tube that would take us directly to Jorok's medical lab.

Once inside, Jorok looked at me with wide eyes and an urgent expression. "Stars," he muttered at the sight of her. "What happened?"

"Blaster hit," I said. "You have got to save her."

He took in the black patch of wound covering with a doubtful eye, but had me set her on the nearest table and got to work. He gestured to the exit. "You've got to leave, Wulfrex," he said. "I can't work with you lurking."

"I can't leave her," I snarled. "She's mine. My mate."

"Clearly," he said. "If you want to save her, let me do my work."

I knew what he was saying, but it didn't make it any easier. My feet were frozen in place. My body was unable to move. An arm swung around my shoulders and a gruff voice spoke in my ear. "Time to go." It was Drave, steering me out of Jorok's medical lab. I didn't resist. I knew logically I had to let Jorok do what he could do. He'd have better luck saving her without me in the way.

Drave brought me back to my quarters, gave me a drink of strong, Heveian ale, and told me to stay the fuck where I was, or he'd lock me in. I barely heard his words. I had no intentions of disturbing Jorok, though. It was out of my hands.

I settled in to my room. There was nothing I could do but wait.

CHAPTER 20

Dani

For the second time, I woke up in the medical lab on the Heveian cruiser. I swear, I was in the same bed as before. But it wasn't Wulfrex staring down at me this time. It was a horrifying face that haunted my dreams. If I had been in any condition other than the state I was in, I would have shrunk away with a whimper.

"Hello, Dani," said Dr. Claire Turich.

But all I could come out with was, "Oh god," and a half-hearted roll to my side. Most of my body felt like it was made of lead.

"She's awake?" I heard Jorok say from across the room.

"Oh, yes," said Claire. "And she remembers me."

I could discern nothing from this woman's expression. She *had* to hate me. I had ended, or at least disrupted, much of her research. Although, I didn't think I had anything to do with her being abducted, like I was. That was just bad luck all around. "Wulfrex," I said in a strangled voice. My throat hurt. Everything hurt.

"He's on his way." Jorok peered down at me, looking satisfied. "You are incredibly resilient. I didn't give you much chance of surviving, but…" He spread his arms. "Here you are."

I groaned. "Joy. Here I am." I looked nervously at Claire. "This is where I should be apologizing, I know. I'm sorry." I hated that I couldn't quite get the defensiveness out of my voice. It wasn't like I killed her partner because I, personally, *wanted* to. The woman had been conspiring with an alien power to acquire weapons that could kill millions.

"You don't need to do that," she said. "I know everything, Dani. Who you are. Why you did what you did." She waved her hand. "Everything."

I closed my eyes. "Wulfrex told everyone?"

"No, I did." A delicate cybot leaned over into my field of vision. Hoc tilted his shiny head. "I sent a relay transmission back to Earth's databanks and got some information on you. We were able to piece together what happened and who you were."

I stifled another groan. "Great. I hear the brig is lovely. I'm looking forward to it."

Jorok frowned. "You're not going to the brig."

"Why not? I'm a murderer You know what I did to

Claire's partner. And it wasn't just her. I killed a lot of people. Most of them deserved it."

"For your job," Claire said. "Yes, we know. Just so you know, I had no idea she was making secret deals behind my back to enrich herself."

"I know that," I said. "If you'd been in on it, you'd be dead too."

Claire sighed. "Well, that's good to know."

There was a commotion at the door, and suddenly everyone was gone and Wulfrex's handsome face filled my vision. His slitted, blue eyes were wide on mine. His pupils were narrow as a knife blade. His dark blue hair was wet and slicked back, secured at the back of his head. He looked haggard, tired. And he looked so happy my heart swelled.

"Dani," he said in a rough voice. "Oh, Dani."

He made to gather me up, but Jorok stopped him with a hand. "Nope. No. She can't be moved, yet. Undo all that hard work I just did and I'll kill you myself."

Wulfrex backed off, but took my hand in his. "You're going to be okay."

"Seems that way." I stared up at him. "Why didn't you tell everybody about me?"

He shrugged. "It wasn't for me to tell. Besides, our Hoc is quite a detective."

I still wasn't quite sure of the cybot. Especially now, after fighting a bunch of them to the death, but there was no denying the difference between Hoc and the ones we encountered. Just like people, there were good and bad.

"When can I get up?" It still concerned me that my body wasn't listening to me.

Jorok once again appeared above me. "I have a block on your nerves from the middle of your chest down, giving your body perfect stillness to heal completely. I had to grow skin, graft it on, and do repairs to some of your organs. It was very touch and go for a while, and you've lost a lot of blood. I gave you an infusion from Arria, whose blood type is compatible with yours. I also used some of Wulfrex's." A smile curved his lips. "So now a little bit of him is also in you."

I returned his smile. "That's the Heveian way, isn't it?"

"Yes," Wulfrex said. "Although the exchange is usually much more pleasurable."

I wanted to laugh, but I couldn't, so I settled for another smile. I could move my hands, so I squeezed his. And that's when I noticed the metal bracelet back on my wrist.

Jorok noticed me looking at it. "No complaints," he said firmly. "You're wearing that until I take it off. And I'm leaving that blocker on your nerves until I get readings showing that your tissues are mended."

"I'm not going to fight you, Doc," I said. "I am grateful to you." I gestured to my motionless body. "For saving me, and all that."

He beamed a smile at me. "It was my pleasure," he said. "I'm very glad I could save you. If not for Wulfrex's quick thinking on the shuttle, closing that wound with the sealing patch, I don't think you would've made it."

"Looks like I owe you another thanks," I said to Wulfrex.

"You owe me nothing. You saved my life, remember?"

"Oh, right. I did." My smile faded as I remembered everything that had happened. "How is that cyborg? And Kiki—the woman that was with him? Are they both okay?"

He nodded. "They're going to be fine. I will have my work cut out for me, giving our cyborg friend some new body parts." He rubbed his hands together. "I can't wait. I've never worked on a cyborg before."

I managed a grainy laugh, and it hurt. "You're adorable," I said to him. "And I'm really not going to the brig?"

He leaned down and pressed his lips to my cheek, then spoke in my ear. "When you are better, you are going to my bed. And you are staying there."

"Right, right," I said. "Until I forget my own name."

He leaned back and rolled his eyes. "I should've known you were listening."

"I'm always listening," I said.

"Then listen now." Thick, calloused fingers slid over my cheek. "I love you. You are my mate, and I'm never letting you go. That's the end of the discussion."

"I guess it's a good thing I love you back, then."

He smiled, wide and radiant. "You'd be crazy not to." And he leaned down and kissed me.

CHAPTER 21

Dani

That wasn't the end. Not by a long shot. The moment Jorok cleared me for "normal everyday life" and removed my vitals monitor, Wulfrex scooped me up in his typical caveman style and hauled me off to his room. It didn't matter to him that I was in mid-sentence with Arria. Nope.

And there's a secret I didn't tell anyone—I loved it. For two full weeks after getting my mobility back, we'd tortured each other with kisses and light make-out sessions. Every time things got heated, my monitor went haywire and Jorok came frantically searching for me.

So by the time it was just us, I was pitifully ready.

We barely made it back to his room before clothing started flying. I didn't even know how my clothes came off, but suddenly I was naked and he was dramatically flinging his pants across the room.

We came together in a clash of bodies and pent-up need. I moaned softly as he kissed my neck and felt his hard body pressed against my own. His hands moved all over my body, greedily caressing my curves and arousing my senses. His touch wasn't gentle or exploratory, but hungry and dominant. For all my bluster about being tough and all, I surrendered to his embrace like a character from a romance novel. It would be pathetic, if I didn't love him so damn much.

His hands moved lower and with a slight pressure, he teased my sex with his calloused fingers. I gasped at the sudden pleasure. My breath quickened as his touch became more insistent, rhythmic, and his own arousal pressed hard and hot against my belly. He moved his hands up my body, testing the weight of my breasts, laving the hard nipples with his tongue.

"Dani." His voice a low, hoarse whisper of desire. His warm breath blew across my skin, sending delicious shivers down my spine. I felt his desire and it matched my own. Our passions rose to a fever pitch as he kissed me deeply. Our tongues entwined in an intimate dance that didn't have to be stopped, this time.

He moved his hands to my hips and with a gentle pressure, drew me closer to him. "Are you sure you're ready?"

"If you back off now, I'll tie you down and take you myself." My body responded to his touch, arching against him as his hands moved over my body.

He chuckled. "We should try that sometime."

Together, we moved to his bed and tumbled on it in a tangle of moans and heated limbs. It was ridiculously large—bigger than a king-sized bed. Later, I'd tease him about getting lost in it, but this was no time for jokes. I felt his arousal. It filled me with delicious pleasure. I moaned softly as his hands moved in tantalizing circles, his lips and tongue following his hands' movements.

He released me from his embrace and gazed into my eyes. I saw the love radiating from his eyes and my heart swelled with joy. He traced my jawline with his fingers, and then moved his hand to cover the large scar that stretched across my abdomen and the hand-sized patch of slightly lighter and softer skin. This was from the graft Jorok had made to cover the wound I should have died from. "I thought I'd lost you."

"I'm tough to kill." The scar wasn't pretty. It also wasn't the only one I had. My body was far from perfect to begin with, and it was also marked by the many missions I'd completed and not come out of unscathed. Now, I saw my body as a tapestry of my life. If I was fortunate, there would be no more scars. No more missions that were supposed to end in someone dying.

I glanced down and watched Wulfrex lean down and press his lips to the scar on my abdomen. He wasn't repulsed by me—not by what I looked like or by what I was. Those fears were gone. He also had a new scar—the hit he took to his thigh was pale silver and raised. I found it profoundly beautiful. "Thank you," I whispered.

He looked up in surprise. "For what?"

"For showing me love," I replied softly, running my fingers through his long blue hair. "For showing me *how* to love. And not in a sappy way."

He grinned. I *loved* his grin, and those long fangs that would bring me pleasure. "I'm never sappy."

I had a snappy quip lined up, but his mouth was on mine and our lips moved in perfect harmony. The intensity of our kiss increased. The warmth of his body and his hands sliding between my legs wiped away all thought. All concerns.

His kisses moved lower and found the hollow of my throat. His tongue caressed my skin and his lips traveled to my breasts. I gasped at the sudden pleasure that flooded my senses as his tongue flicked my aching nipples and he suckled gently. He kissed and caressed lower, even lower. I spread my legs and he buried his face in my pussy, laving my aching folds until I thought I would explode with pleasure.

Until I *did* explode with pleasure.

Satisfied with himself, he kissed his way back up to my neck. He pulled me closer. His arousal was impossibly hard. "Are you sure?"

"Stop asking me that," I said. "If I wasn't sure I wouldn't be here." My body arched towards him and my desire grew with every movement. I wrapped my hand around his engorged cock and squeezed. "Does it *seem* like I'm not sure?"

He chuckled and shifted us both so I lay on my back and he loomed over me, huge and possessive. He moved his fingertips over my body, exploring my curves and arousing my senses. His touch was tender and passionate. I melted into him.

————

"Okay, then," he said huskily. "No taking it back."

Our eyes met in a passionate gaze. My heart raced and I felt a wave of warmth wash over me. Our tongues entwined in an intimate dance. His hands braced on either side of me. His knees shoved my legs apart and he settled between them.

His cock nudged the folds of my sex, pressing forward. His hips angled forward, impaling himself in my hot, needy pussy. "Oh, fuck yes."

Our love-making built in passion as our desires rose to an almost unbearable intensity. He moved inside me and I gasped at the sudden pleasure that filled my body. His movements were gentle and controlled, yet passionate and intense. We moved together in perfect harmony, lost in our own desires. When his fangs found their way to my neck, I was squirming with anticipation.

I trembled with pleasure as a fresh wave of it moved through me like liquid indulgence. His name escaped my lips in a gasp. My body clenched as passion rocked through me like a torrent. I bucked against him, demanding more. *Needing* more.

I wrapped my legs around his hips. Pleasure pulsed hard and thick through me as I came, milking his cock as he pounded, hard and fast. I cried out his name as I exploded, coming hard and wild and flooded with emotions I could barely understand. He found his own release with a shuddering groan and gathered me against him.

His warmth and his love washed over me as we lay together, our bodies still intertwined.

"Mine." He kissed me softly. "All mine."

"Yours," I breathed.

He looked up at me. "I'm serious, you know. You're mine now. My mate. It's not a thing that can be undone."

I propped myself up on one elbow. "Let me tell you something. I've been yours from the beginning. From when I first opened my eyes and found you staring down at me with these gorgeous eyes." I brushed trembling fingers over his eyebrow and he closed his eyes. "I just didn't know it, then."

We held each other close, settling in to the nearness and warmth of one another. We lay together in harmony. It was the first time I'd ever felt such a thing. Our hearts and bodies were in perfect unity, and the love that we shared filled everything around us.

The intensity of the moment slowly eased. We lay there in a comfortable silence until I felt his arms soften around me and his breathing turn deep and steady. All my fears and worries melted away. I was his, yes. But he was also mine. In that moment, I knew that no matter what else life threw at us, nothing could break us apart. We had found each other and were now linked in a bond that was unbreakable.

CHAPTER 22

Dani

"You were a spy." Harp blinked at me. "That's badass, dude."

"It wasn't as glamorous as you're thinking." I took a scoop of ice cream with their newly tested hot fudge.

"Did you have to kill people?"

"Harp, that's not a good question," said Kora, sending me a worried look.

"S'okay," I said around a mouthful. "I'd rather answer questions than have you all wondering." I nodded to Harp. "Yeah, I did."

"A lot of people?"

"Harp!" Kora smacked her arm.

"Yup." I looked at her. "But don't worry. I'm not going to kill anyone on this ship."

It was only the four of us—Kora, Harp, Arria, and

me, eating ice cream and sipping wine. The two surprisingly worked together. Space had been made by clearing out storage for Claire and Kiki to have their own room. They went to bed early, as a rule. When they joined us for ice cream night, they spent half of it yawning. Arria was more of a night owl.

"No one?" Harp pressed, but with a grin.

"Not even Claire," I said with an eye roll.

"Did you ever think about it?" Arria scooped up a spoonful of just fudge and ate it. "I know you were worried what she'd say when she woke up."

"Actually, no. I didn't." I scraped fudge from the side of the bowl. "This still feels a little rubbery on my tongue."

"I know," said Kora. "It still needs work. I thought we had it, but no."

"I felt bad for her," I said. For some reason, I wasn't ready to let the topic go. "The last thing she saw before we were both taken, was me standing over her dead partner. She must have been terrified." I shrugged. "And I worried what you'd think of me."

"You worried what we'd think?" asked Arria, as if it was a surprise.

"Of course." I stared at her. "Women can be really mean to each other. On this ship, there's only a few of us. I didn't want you all turning on me." I frowned and shoved more ice cream in my mouth. "That would have been miserable."

Kora shook her head. "We wouldn't turn on you. Ever."

"Yeah. We don't want to get offed in our sleep," said Harp, who winked at me.

Arria gave Harp a pained look. "That was dark, Harp. I didn't like that."

"I'm sorry, Arria." Harp looked instantly contrite. "It was a joke. A very bad one." She looked at me. "Apologies, Dani."

I waved a hand. "It's fine." Really, it was. I could hardly be sensitive about it at this point.

Arria nodded, mollified. "We all come from different worlds," she said thoughtfully. "But we're all here." She looked at each of us with warmth in her eyes. "You're all my family, you know. *All* of you."

That last bit was for my benefit, and it felt good, hearing her say that. "I'm not a spy anymore," I said. "It was time to quit, anyway. I'm thirty, now. Not as fast. Not as sharp." I rubbed my chin. "I wonder if they would have *let* me leave."

"What could they have done if they decided you wouldn't be allowed to leave?" Harp wanted to know.

I gave her a level look and shook my head. "Um. Can you guess?"

Harp let out a whistle. "I thought they were tough in the military."

"I'm glad I wound up here, instead," I said, setting my empty bowl aside. "Because you all are my family, too. I didn't have one on Earth."

"Now you have us *and* Wulfrex." Kora pulled her hair up in a messy bun. "He's such a dish."

I chuckled. "Yes. He knows."

Kora's face turned serious. "I wanted to ask you something. Ryland said something about when you were in that alien laboratory, in the mine. He said the Kloog you were questioning said Earth already belonged to the UCP. What else did he say about that?"

"Ah." I leaned back in the cushioned seat. "I don't know if that little creature was just trying to push buttons or if that was accurate. You three have been to our home planet more recently than I have. Does it appear to have been taken over by outside forces?"

Harp pressed her lips together. "I don't know, to be honest. Tech moved faster than light, it seemed. Every month we were getting upgraded equipment and devices." She rolled her eyes. "*Training* for the new equipment and devices. It's impossible to know what was going on behind the scenes."

"Claire would be a better one to ask," said Kora. "But she doesn't like to talk about her work before, well, *before*."

"And Kiki was a student," said Arria. "Still, I should ask her about it." Arria and Kiki had bonded over their love of learning and ability to learn *fast*. Both fell into the genius category, making them very interesting and eccentric.

"Hoc can do some work on that, too," I said. I'd come to a peace with the cybot. He'd grown on me over the past month as I'd healed. Every day, he'd come to see me, asking me if I needed anything. When I was stuck in the medical lab's bed, he stayed with me when Wulfrex had to step away. He'd tell stories and jokes. It was impossible to dislike the guy. My mate adored him, constantly tweaking this and that on his metal body. He added new wrist joints so Hoc could rotate them in a wider circumference. It was ridiculous. I'd never seen a cybot more pampered than this one.

There was noise in the hall.

"Which one do you think it is?" Harp asked. "Not my Drave. He's so silent it's creepy."

Kora shrugged. "Ryland is training the maintenance crew on electrical spears tonight."

"That would be Wulf, then." I rose and stretched as the door opened and my huge, handsome Heveian sauntered inside.

"Hello, females," he said with a jaunty smile. "How is the fudge coming along?"

Kora shook her head. "Not there, yet."

"Ah, pity. I look forward to trying it one day." He was interested in trying Earth food, but didn't want to eat any that didn't taste like the real thing.

"You'll love it," said Harp. "Dani, get an eyeful now because once your man gets a taste of ice cream with hot fudge, you can kiss those abs goodbye."

"They're not dairy," Arria reminded her. "Not fattening."

"Right. I forgot." Harp shrugged and took another spoonful. "Want to take some to go?" she asked me.

Wulfrex walked up to me and scooped me into his arms. "Another time," he said. "I intend to keep Dani's mouth occupied for the next few hours."

My face warmed as Harp let out a whistle and Arria

groaned. I waved as he carried me away like an ogre having just pillaged a village and carrying off his prize. "You're terrible," I said into his neck as he strode down the hall.

"You will be eating those words in a few minutes," he said, lowering his head and nipping my earlobe. "Among other things."

I laughed, because I loved the guy, and my body was heating at his words and touch. I wrapped my arms around his thick neck and breathed in his scent. There was nowhere else I wanted to be. No one else I wanted to spend my life with.

He opened the door and carried me inside. "I can make you ice cream, if you want."

"No," I said, gazing adoringly into his light, catlike eyes. "All I want right now is you."

"That is yours," he said. "All yours. Forever."

EPILOGUE

"There. Try that." I leaned away from the Heveian cyborg who sat patiently in my workshop as I attached the final bits to his new leg. I raised my hands and he experimentally raised it and bent the knee, then the ankle. It worked like a normal leg, rather than the hulking monstrosity the Kloog scientists had burdened him with.

He looked at me with surprise. "Works," he said.

"Of course, it does." I wiped some fusion grease from my fingers. "You'll need to see me for mainte-nance. Anything feels loose or sticks, come find me."

"Thank-ss." The cyborg, whose name we learned was Craal, had his vocal and comprehension capabili-ties restored, thanks to Jorok. He'd *just* gotten these back, though, so he was still working on making the connections for speech. The Kloog aliens had ravaged him. They'd loaded him up with neurological implants in an effort to control him entirely, and in addition to cutting off his ability to speak, they'd blocked his memories.

Jorok wasn't done with him, yet. There were still more things to remove from his brain, and other things to fix. I wasn't done with him, either. I'd begun by giving him a proper leg before working on an arm, so he could get around easier.

"It's a work of art, Wulf," said Axlos, who appeared in the doorway. "Looks like a real leg."

"Made of metal, yes." I examined the curved calf and carefully crafted toes I'd made. "I could hide the seams a little better, if you'd like."

Craal shook his head. "Good." His lips turned up at the corners. "Good," he said again.

I nodded. "Okay, then. Why don't you give it a try? Go walk around the cruiser a bit. You know, break it in."

He looked quizzically at me for a moment, reminding me that the terms we'd picked up from the humans didn't make sense to anyone other than them. And now, us.

He rose and put weight on the leg, testing it out. His one eye blinked rapidly as he began to comprehend that he would be walking more normally now and not with a gross limp from a metal limb that didn't fit him. He smiled again, more fully, and dropped a hand on my shoulder. He nodded, refraining from saying "good" for a third time, and walked out of my workshop with a normal stride.

I sat back, pleased with my work. "Go ahead and say it," I said to Axlos. "You know you want to."

He raised one brow. "What do I want to say?"

"That I'm a mechanical genius." I spread my arms with a grin. "I'm an irreplaceable and invaluable member of this crew."

He grunted at me and sat on a crate of parts. "I'm not saying it."

I laughed. "Fine. But you're thinking it."

He raised one brow. "That female of yours is making your head swell."

"Nah, it was always this big."

Axlos smiled, which was an accomplishment these days. His mind was busy—worrying over the next move the UCP was going to make, worrying about the females on the ship, and now, worrying about the cyborg Heveian who was just beginning to regain his memories. "That really was good work," he said. "Will you start working on his arm next?"

I shrugged. "I'm going to give him the option of the arm or his eye next. We can do better than a metal patch over it."

"You're going to make that male a new *eye?*"

"Why not?" I rolled my shoulders, which were stiff after working for so long on the leg. "It can't be that hard. It's a mechanical device, like any other. I'll have to coordinate with Jorok on that, though, with eyes being so close to the brain."

Axlos shook his head. "You *are* a genius, you know."

"Ah." I smiled serenely. "I knew you wanted to say it."

"I don't know how she lives with you."

"I make Dani so happy, she doesn't mind my occasional gloating," I said.

"Occasional?"

"I could do it more—"

He held up a hand. "We're good. Thanks. Look, I came here to talk to you about something."

"Yeah?"

"Dani said that the female she was ordered to kill was a scientist who was working with the UCP," he said. "That means they were meddling in human affairs more than fifty years ago."

"Ah." I ran my hands through my hair.

"Which means Earth might be lost to them, if they infiltrated deeply enough."

My gut sank. "Which means our females may not ever be able to visit their home planet."

"Or return there permanently, if they choose," Axlos said. "It wouldn't be safe."

"Dani is staying," I said, and I knew that because we'd discussed it many times over the past month. It was a conversation we would continue to have, but the longer we were together, the closer and deeper our bond was becoming. "So are Harp and Kora, I'm sure. Arria wants to go to Heveia. The other two, I have no idea."

"Right." Axlos winced. "About the other two. One is

a high-value scientist who's been missing for fifty-two years and the other is…the crown princess' sister."

I wasn't surprised easily, but that one had my jaw dropping. "No way."

"Yes. Kiki is Princess Lila's sister."

I pushed away with my chair and the roller balls on the bottom sent me gliding across the cramped and cluttered space. "Fuck."

Axlos nodded. "My thoughts, too."

"Does Lila know?"

"Not a clue. She hasn't had contact with anyone from Earth since her own abduction. We have to assume her sister was taken for the same reason Lila was— because of the unique qualities in her blood. But once the cure was found, she was no longer needed."

"That explains why the Kloog alien scientists didn't do anything with her," I said. "Those instructions were revoked so she just…languished in that cell."

"The Kloogs probably thought their prisoners would kill her and be done with it."

"But no," I said. "Craal kept her alive. They kept each other alive." I shook my head. "There doesn't seem to be any sort of mate bond between them. I think they were just…what? Friends?"

"It appears that way. They bonded, but not sexually. According to Jorok, there's nothing wrong with Craal physically. Nothing prevents him from rutting, or inhibits the desire to rut. They're just not mates."

"It would be hard to mate with those metal parts," I

said, thoughtfully. "Maybe now that he has more mobility..."

Axlos shook his head. "They're *not* mates. The other females deduced that easily enough. She's like a sister to him and she sees him in the same light."

"Interesting." I let out a whistle. "Crown Prince Gavrox is going to shit himself when he finds out that we have the sister of his mate on our ship."

"He will not be pleased by the conditions the female was found in." Axlos leaned back, stretching his back and letting out a long sigh. This, now, *finally*, was what he came here to talk about. Everything up until now was background information. "We need to end the UCP," he said. "Once and for all. For good."

I let out the air in my lungs slowly. "How do you propose we do that? You know our population is barely a million. We lack people and equipment to battle an organization that big."

"We have proof of their deeds," he said. "We need to make everyone see it."

"Some won't care."

"Many will."

"No." I rose to my feet and paced the small space. "There needs to be more than that."

Axlos smiled at me, as if proud that I'd gotten an answer right. "What does the UCP want?"

"From us? The *vistran* beneath the surface of Heveia," I replied. "In general? Power, I guess."

"Domination can be had by controlling the greatest power source in the galaxy."

"So what do you propose we do?"

A smile spread on Axlos' face. A wide, wise smile that had the ability to ease the most worried minds. "We distribute the *vistran*. Everywhere. We sell, of course, but low enough that every system can purchase it. We *don't* sell it to any UCP-controlled worlds."

"That won't be easy."

"I never said it would be."

I scratched my head. "And you think Gavrox will go along with this?"

"After he learns what Kiki and Craal have been through? Yes."

"What do the others think?" I asked, wondering for the first time why all five of us weren't in this room talking about it together.

"I'll talk about it with them after we're done," said Axlos. "You, of all of us, have a mind that can analyze problems and find solutions to them. Jorok, too, but his mind is occupied. If you followed my thinking and agreed, it was a plan worth trying on."

I nodded thoughtfully. "It could fail very easily. The UCP could intercept shipments, bully worlds into giving up theirs. They could simply declare war on Heveia."

"They could."

I thought it all over in my head, turning it around like a broken mechanical device that needed fixing. "An awful lot of pieces need to fit together."

He smiled. "That's why we have you, Wulfrex."

Hi readers! I hope you enjoyed Wulfrex and Dani's story! Please consider leaving a review. This is the third book in the Craving the Heveian series. For free stories, bonus content, and book news, sign up for my newsletter at ellablakeauthor.com

The Alien's Escape is releasing next. Jorok meets a fiery match of his own and gets thrust into a surprising quest with Kiki that uncovers the true origin of the UCP...and how to begin upending it.

So, I have the hots for my alien doctor.

Jorok saved my life after being trapped in a filthy cell. He's gorgeous and way too serious for his own good. To get to know him better, I tag along on an errand, but we're kidnapped and forced to nurse an alien captain's sick crew. To avoid being sold, I pretend to be Jorok's mate (which isn't difficult). I thought things couldn't get worse from there. I was wrong.

Kiki is utterly delectable. She's brilliant, amusing, and beautiful, but she's also my queen's sister and deserves someone who can devote more time to her. Which I can't, since I'm a physician to the ship's entire crew. When she and I travel to a merchant city for supplies, we're taken by a band of Gutturians who want me to cure their crew of a mystery sickness. A deathbed confession sets us off on a quest to uncover the source of the oppressive group who is determined to wipe out my people…and hers. Kiki's intoxicating charms are the least of my problems…and one I can no longer resist.

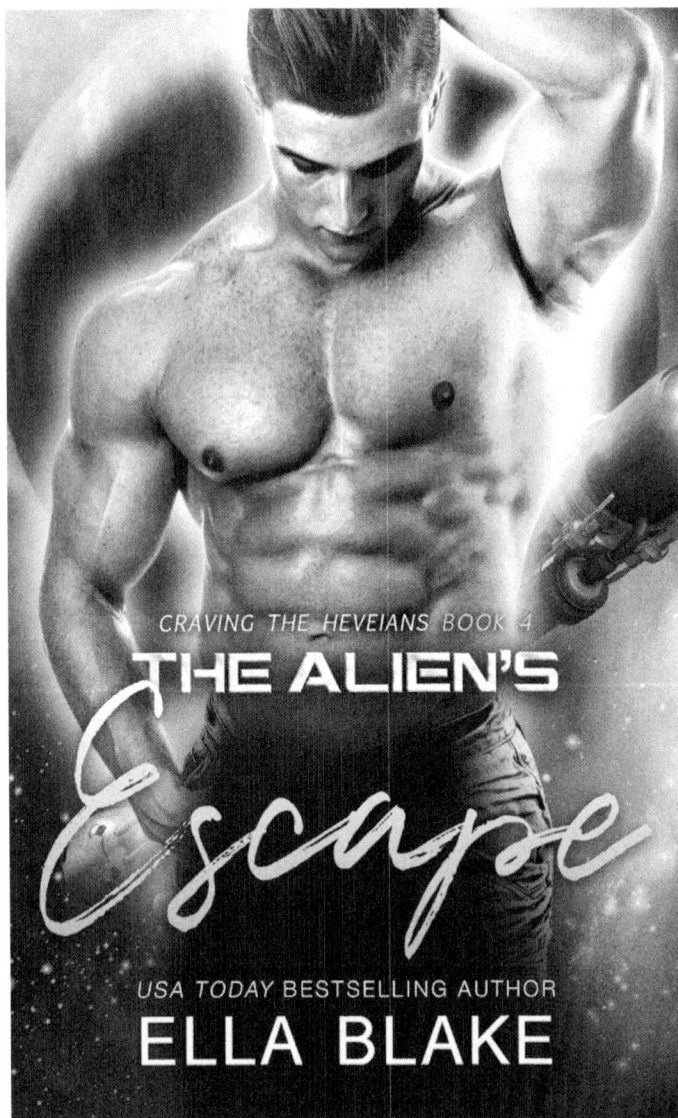

CRAVING THE HEVEIANS BOOK 4

THE ALIEN'S

Escape

USA TODAY BESTSELLING AUTHOR

ELLA BLAKE

ALSO BY ELLA BLAKE

Craving the Heveians

VIRGO'S PRIZE

THE ALIEN'S BITE

THE ALIEN'S FIRE

THE ALIEN'S BLADE

THE ALIEN'S ESCAPE

Stryxian Alien Warriors

BONDED TO THE STRYXIAN

STRANDED WITH THE STRYXIAN (free novella)

SAVED BY THE STRYXIAN

CLAIMED BY THE STRYXIAN

POSSESSED BY THE STRYXIAN

CHAINED TO THE STRYXIAN

SEDUCED BY THE STRYXIAN

The Lords of Destra

LOST TO THE ALIEN LORD

BOUND TO THE ALIEN LORD

FATED TO THE ALIEN LORD

CRAVED BY THE ALIEN LORD

DESTINED FOR THE ALIEN LORD

ENSNARED BY THE ALIEN LORD

Virilian Mail Order Mates

TRAK

DREX

VIRAK

NIIR

TARON

KIM & KLAE (novella)

SAKAR (bonus holiday book)

The Baylan Chronicles

DRACE

RAZE

ARTEN

HARC

ZADE